VELVET CAKE AND MURDER

A SANDY BAY COZY MYSTERY

AMBER CREWES

PEN-N-A-PAD PUBLISHING

A SANDY BAY COZY MYSTERY

BOOK TWENTY-TWO

The tiny snowflakes looked like diamonds as they fell from the sky, each glittering as they floated into the glowing path of the street light positioned outside of the bakery door. It was a bitterly cold winter morning, but the beauty of the snow was enough to take Meghan Truman Irvin's mind off of the cold.

Meghan didn't like the cold. As a native of a warm, small town in Texas, she had moved to sunny Los Angeles following her college graduation. Never in a million years had she expected to find herself living in the Pacific Northwest, but now, here she was. She adored her adopted hometown, a little seaside oasis called Sandy Bay, and had followed her dream of owning and operating her own bakery. A few weeks after moving to town, she had met the love of her life in Sandy Bay, the town detective. Meghan had recently gotten married and was happily beginning her married life in the town she had grown to love so dearly.

Meghan unlocked the door of Truly Sweet, the bakery she had opened in Sandy Bay after moving from Los Angeles almost three years ago. The little silvery bells attached to the front door chimed as she walked in, and she smiled in spite of herself; the sound of those little bells always brought her so much joy, and after a few years of owning and operating the bakery, she couldn't believe she got to do something she loved every single day.

"Hey," she heard a voice from behind her, and she turned to greet Pamela, the teenager who worked for her part-time.

"Good morning," she smiled warmly. "You look sleepy!"

Pamela yawned. "It's Saturday morning," she moaned as she kicked the snow off of her boots on the indoor welcome mat. "I should be sleeping in or having a lazy breakfast."

"Or getting paid to bake," Trudy, Meghan's middle-aged employee, grunted as she walked in behind her. "Kids your age need to be working, or you get into trouble."

Pamela rolled her eyes. "That's what my mom says…"

Meghan chuckled. "Your mom is right," she agreed. "How about this, sleepy head? Let's put in two good hours of work, and then we can take a long break for an early lunch?"

Trudy smiled. "Sounds good, boss."

"Only if I can have a hot scone," Pamela grinned.

"I think we can make that happen!" Meghan nodded, and the three ladies set to work preparing the bakery for the day.

Exactly two hours later, Pamela cleared her throat loudly. "Meghan?"

Meghan glanced down at the watch on her wrist. "You were watching the clock, weren't you?" she laughed as she wiped her hands on her apron and started piling dishes in the sink in the kitchen.

"I really want my hot, fresh scone," Pamela smiled, nodding at the oven, which had just gone off. "And the timing is perfect."

Meghan laughed. "I'll get your scone and some tea assembled. Why don't you two go wait for me in the dining room?"

Ten minutes later, Meghan walked out to the dining room with a tray of scones, breakfast tea, cream, and sugar. Trudy and Pamela were waiting for her at one of the little white iron tables in the corner, and she set the treats down with a flourish. "Ta da!"

Pamela inhaled dramatically. "Ahhhhh," she moaned happily, closing her eyes and smiling as the smell of the hot scones wafted through the air. "I'm ready to chow down!"

Trudy cocked her head toward the platter. "I think I'll take two," she said sheepishly, and Meghan nodded.

"Take as many as you'd like," she urged. "I made more than we'll sell today, all just for you."

They settled down and relaxed; it was a slow morning at the bakery, and as the snow fell outside, Meghan felt cozy and grateful to be starting what she hoped to be another successful year. The previous year had had many high points. She got married, went on a memorable honeymoon, settled into married life, and had grown her business more than she ever could have dreamed. While she was sad to say goodbye to such a fun, happy year, she was eager for all that was to come in the year ahead.

"Maybe I shouldn't eat this," Pamela sniffed at the scone, bringing Meghan's attention back to the conversation.

"You wanted it," Trudy insisted. "What's the problem?"

Pamela looked down at her feet. "My New Year's resolution is to lose some weight," she explained. "If I want to look good in my swimsuit for the spring swim season, I need to shed a few pounds."

Meghan slammed her hand down on the table. "Enough of that talk," she ordered. "Pamela, you are *perfect*; you are tall and muscular, and you have a figure that many women would kill for."

"You do," Trudy agreed. "And you have the metabolism of a teenager. Enjoy it now, honey. It won't last forever."

"But Roberto's new girlfriend is stick-thin," Pamela complained, leaning back and crossing her arms over her small bosom. "Maybe if I were skinnier, we would get back together."

Meghan stood up and put her hands on her curvy hips. Meghan and Pamela were built completely differently; while Pamela was statuesque and blonde, Meghan was petite, with prominent, feminine curves and dark hair that cascaded down her back in luscious waves. She hadn't always liked her womanly figure, but as she grew up, and had come to appreciate the way her clothes hung on her hourglass body, and while she knew she would never be a supermodel, she knew she was pretty on the inside and the outside.

"Listen to me," she demanded as Pamela stared at her. "Your body is perfect. You are so beautiful, and hard-working, and smart, and responsible. You do not need to change anything about yourself, okay?"

"She's right," Trudy agreed. "I know I give you a hard time sometimes, but that's because I have high expectations of you. You are a great girl, and you don't need to change anything about yourself."

Pamela smiled. "Thanks," she said softly. "That means a lot to me."

Meghan sat back down and wrapped her arm around Pamela's shoulder. "Now, do you have any real resolutions?" she asked kindly. "Mine is to stretch out before and after my runs so my legs don't cramp up!"

"That's a good one," Pamela nodded. "You really like running now, don't you?"

Meghan shrugged. "I'll never make it to the Olympics," she smiled. "But I enjoy a good run to clear my head and move my body."

Trudy cleared her throat. "I want to share my resolution."

"What is it?" Meghan asked.

"I want to learn Portuguese," Trudy grinned, her eyes sparkling. "I was watching Love Actually over the holidays, and that guy who speaks Portuguese is such a cutie."

Meghan laughed. "You like that Portuguese guy? Hugh Grant is more my style."

"Hugh Grant?" Pamela wondered. "Who is that? I've never heard of him."

Trudy shook her head. "You don't know who Hugh Grant is?"

"Does he have a YouTube channel?"

Meghan closed her eyes. "Oh, Pamela…"

They chatted for a few more minutes, and then Meghan turned her attention toward her business. "What are your goals for the next year at Truly Sweet?" she first asked Trudy.

"I want to do more baking," she told Meghan. "I like my role as a manager, but I want to get better at the baking. Pamela is a third of my age, but she can bake better than me. I want to get on her level."

Meghan laughed. "It isn't a competition," she assured Trudy. "And you do an amazing job managing the bakery, I promise."

Pamela bit her lip. "What should my goal be?" she asked.

Meghan thought for a moment. "What if we do some swaps this year?" she suggested. "Trudy can learn more about baking from you, and she can teach you more about managing the bakery. I think that would make you a really well-rounded employee, and it would look good on your college applications."

"Okay," Pamela agreed. "That's probably a good idea."

"What are your goals for the bakery?" Trudy asked Meghan. "We did so well last year, and I can't imagine that will change in the year ahead."

Meghan pondered the question. Should she maintain the

norms of the bakery? Things were going really well; they nearly had more orders than they could handle, and Meghan was even considering hiring another part-time employee to help out on weekday mornings when Pamela was at school.

"Maybe we should shake things up," Pamela suggested. "It never hurts to try new things."

Meghan nodded. Besides a new employee, what else could they incorporate at the bakery? They always rotated new treats in and out, the menu changed constantly, and Meghan had just had the dining room walls painted a new color: blush.

"What about some new furniture for the dining room?" Pamela asked. "We could go shopping in Portland. I am really good at design and aesthetics."

Meghan furrowed her brow. "I'm not quite sure about that," she told Pamela. "I'll think about it."

They finished their snacks and returned to work, Meghan still thinking about her goals and aspirations for the bakery. Should she implement some changes, or should she keep the status quo? She could not decide, and she decided to bring it up with her husband, Jack, when she got home later.

That evening, Meghan was exhausted and filthy as she arrived home. A group of five children and a frantic father had shown up at the bakery before closing; the father had promised his children donuts if they behaved while his wife was at the grocery, and when he realized the bakery did not have donuts on the current menu, he had given Meghan attitude. The children had screamed and moaned, but finally, she was able to pacify them with cinnamon bagels and cinnamon sugar frosting.

Walking into her house, and smiling as Fiesta and Siesta, her two little twin dogs, ran to greet her. "Hi, babies," she said, reaching down to scoop them up into her arms.

"Hey!" Jack grinned as he strode into the living room.

While Meghan was exhausted, she was happy to see her husband; he was a detective with the Sandy Bay Police, and their schedules had not allowed them to spend much time together after Christmas.

"Hi, honey," she murmured as she kissed him on the lips. "How was your day?"

"Well, I have something to tell--"

"My day was wild," she told him, pulling away from his embrace so she could remove her winter coat. "We did some goal setting in the morning, and then, there was a huge rush at the end of the day."

"Meghan? Can we chat?"

"In a minute," she waved him off. "I want to tell you about the goal setting. Anyway, Trudy wants us to keep with the status quo at the bakery, but Pamela really wants to shake things up. What do you think about that?"

Meghan hung her coat up on the coat rack as Dash, their other dog, bounded into the room. "Hi, buddy," she said as she bent down to scratch his ears. "Anyway, the conversation got me thinking about our goals as a couple."

Jack raised an eyebrow. "Our goals as a couple?"

"Exactly," she nodded. "What are our goals as a couple this year? I think we need to work a little harder on our communication. Remember that argument we had about the boys' night? If we had just communicated about it, things would have been fine."

"Meghan, I need to talk to you," Jack interrupted, but Meghan kept talking.

"What if we commit to reading a book together each month?" she suggested as she threw herself onto the couch and put her feet up on the oak coffee table. "A relationship book or something about financial freedom? I hear a lot of young couples make mistakes with their money and maybe learning more about finances could be one of our goals."

"Meghan," Jack interjected.

"What?" she asked. "Why are you interrupting me? I just want to talk about all the ways I want us to be a better couple. Doesn't that matter to you?"

Jack laughed. "Meghan, of course it matters to me!" he exclaimed, coming to sit next her on the couch. "I just need to tell you something."

"What?"

There was suddenly a knock on the front door. "Who could that be?" Meghan asked, frowning as she crossed her arms over her chest. "Are you expecting someone?"

Jack had a sheepish look on his face. "I was trying to tell you," he sighed as he rose to his feet and made his way to the door.

Meghan bit her lip. "Who is it?" she asked, standing up and walking over to him. "Who is at the door, Jack?"

2

"My dearest! My little Jacky-pie!"

Meghan's ears hurt as a screeching voice filled the living room. She glanced over her husband's broad shoulders and stifled a gasp. It was Sarah Irvin, her mother-in-law. She was holding three suitcases and was balancing a duffle bag on her shoulders.

"And my new daughter!"

Sarah pushed her way inside and threw her arms around Meghan, dropping the bags and giving her two kisses on each cheek. "Look at you, Meghan! You look like you've put on some weight! Are you pregnant? You're just glowing! Is my first grandson on the way?"

"It must be that first year of marriage glow," Meghan laughed weakly. "No grandchildren yet, Sarah."

Jack led his mother into the living room. "Meghan, I was trying to tell you," he murmured, flashing her an apologetic look. "Mom is going to be with us for a few days."

"A few days?" Sarah cried. "More like a few weeks! Your father's fishing trips in British Columbia are always so long, and I hate being home by myself. Besides, I haven't seen you two since your wedding, and your dear mom needs to visit with her darlings."

Meghan's stomach dropped. A few weeks? She was busier than ever at the bakery, and she was still exhausted from the holiday season.

"You look so surprised, Meghan!" Sarah commented. "Aren't you excited to have your mother-in-law in town? I remember loving the visits Jack's father and I used to have with his mother when she was still alive. Those visits were the highlights of our early married life."

Meghan forced herself to smile. "I'm just tired from a long day at work," she explained. "Of course we are happy you are here. Can I get you something to drink? A snack?"

Sarah smiled. "Jack told me on the phone that you were making a nice dinner for my arrival."

Meghan turned to glower at her husband. "What is going on?" she mouthed, but Sarah came and wrapped her in a hug.

"Thank you so much for hosting your dear old mother-in-law," she told Meghan. "It is so sweet of you. I knew Jack made the right choice when he married you. His ex-girlfriend, Nina, was so unpleasant to be around. She hated when I would drop in or stay for a few weeks, and I am so glad you are different."

Meghan nodded politely, but then turned to her husband. "Can you help me get dinner started?" she asked in a stiff tone.

"Of course," he replied nervously, and they walked into the kitchen, leaving Sarah sitting on the couch.

"What is going on?" Meghan whispered as Jack closed the door. "Were you going to tell me about this?"

"I tried!" he insisted. "When you got home from work. She called me this morning and told me she was coming."

"Then why didn't you call me at work and tell me?" she hissed, putting her hands on her hips. "We don't have

12

anything ready! The house isn't clean, we don't have groceries. And it's your night to cook dinner. And why is she telling me about your ex-girlfriend? I don't need to hear it."

Jack put his hands on her shoulders, his bright blue eyes staring into hers. "Hey," he muttered. "I'm sorry. I'm sorry that things got out of control. She didn't really ask; she just told me she was coming. I should have called you immediately."

"Yeah, you should have," she pulled away from him. "Why don't you go entertain her? I guess I have a dinner I'm supposed to make…"

The next morning, Meghan was late arriving at the bakery. She had hardly slept the night before; Sarah had insisted that she take Meghan and Jack's bedroom, and the couple had had to sleep on the pullout couch in the living room. The couch bed was small and lumpy, and with all three dogs piled atop them, Meghan and Jack had barely gotten any sleep.

"You're late," Trudy commented as Meghan walked into the dining room. "And you look like a mess. Look at those bags under your eyes."

Meghan rubbed at her face and yawned. "I didn't sleep last night."

"Clearly," Trudy chuckled. "What's wrong? Troubles at the Irvin house?"

"It's an Irvin problem," Meghan agreed.

"What did Jack do?" Trudy asked. "Did he leave the toilet seat up again?"

Meghan shook her head. "It isn't Jack," she corrected Trudy. "It's Sarah. His mother. She's in town, and she's staying at our house."

Trudy raised an eyebrow. "Did you know about this? You didn't tell me she was coming to stay."

Meghan huffed. "I had no idea," she told her. "Jack said

she called yesterday morning and told him she was coming for several weeks. When I got home from work, she showed up with a bunch of bags."

Trudy shuddered. "That sounds awful," she told Meghan. "I hate having houseguests. I can't imagine having ones that stay that long…"

Meghan shrugged. "I don't think that's the worst of it," she sighed. "Sarah is nice, but she is so passive-aggressive. She constantly makes these little side comments about us not visiting her, us not calling her, and all the things she didn't like about our wedding, including my dress."

"So, she isn't overly mean?"

"I guess not," Meghan admitted. "But the comments just keep adding up. It's really driving me nuts."

Trudy laughed. "My mother-in-law, God rest her soul, was downright mean," she told Meghan. "She would say mean things about my looks, my cooking, and my house. I don't think she ever had a nice word to say about me. It must be some sort of rule for mothers-in-law to be dreadful."

Meghan joined her behind the counter. "That does sound difficult," she agreed. "Thank goodness I have to work today; she was up at dawn and already dropping hints about having a big breakfast made for her, but I had to hurry up and get out of the house for work."

Trudy gestured at the row of cakes displayed in the counter. "Speaking of work," she began. "I was thinking about the goal setting we talked about yesterday, and I had an idea."

"What is it?"

"The wedding market," Trudy beamed. "My niece is getting married next month, and I asked her about her cake. Meghan, brides pay thousands of dollars for wedding cakes and treats! What if we break into the wedding market this year?"

Just then, the front door of the bakery opened. Meghan shivered as a gust of cold air hit her face.

"Good morning!"

Anthony Diggs, a local businessman, greeted them with his megawatt smile. Anthony was young, energetic, and handsome; rumor around town was that he was planning to run for mayor, and with his good looks and sparkling personality, he was often called a "young John F. Kennedy."

"Anthony," Meghan smiled as he approached the counter. "How are you today?"

He licked his lips good naturedly. "I'm hungry," he told her.

"Then you're in the right place," Trudy giggled, blushing as he bent down to examine the desserts in the display case.

"What can we do for you today?" Meghan asked. "How's Bonnie?"

Anthony stood back up. "The wife is better than ever," he told them. "Though she would be a bit better if I came home today with a cupcake for her. Do you have any recommendations?"

"Our red velvet cupcakes are our newest flavor," Trudy informed him as she pointed to the delicate red desserts artfully arrangement in the case. "We debuted them over Thanksgiving weekend, and they've been selling like crazy!"

Anthony's face lit up. "That sounds like something she would love. I'll take twelve."

"Twelve?" Trudy exclaimed as Anthony nodded.

"My staff would love them; I'll take enough to make my wife happy *and* my employees happy."

Meghan started wrapping up cupcakes and placing them in a festive red box. "Thank you so much for stopping by," she told him as she placed the box in his hands.

"You've helped me so much, Meghan," he told her, leaning

in as Trudy went back to the kitchen. "You've helped keep my office happy and my wife in a sweet mood."'

"That's my job!" she chirped.

Anthony narrowed his eyes. "Look, I wasn't really coming in to get dessert," he whispered as Meghan's dark eyes widened. "Can I ask you a favor?"

Meghan pursed her lips. She knew Anthony in passing, but they were not good friends. What could he possibly want from her?

"What do you mean?" she asked, whispering so the customers in the dining room wouldn't hear.

He swallowed, took a deep breath, and stared into her eyes. "My life kind of depends on it," he began, and she felt her stomach churn. "I'm in trouble, and I need your help."

What was he talking about? Did she even *want* to know? Meghan did not know, but as she stood in the dining room of Truly Sweet, she had a feeling things were about to go wrong.

3

M eghan's heart beat furiously in her chest as Anthony stared at her. "What is it?" she asked, leaning in toward him.

He glanced around to make sure no one was listening. "I know this is kind of an open secret," he murmured under his breath. "But in case you hadn't heard, I am running for Mayor."

Meghan nodded. "I've heard that," she whispered. "You are right: it is not much of a secret, Anthony."

He smiled. "Secrets are hard to keep in this town."

She peered at him curiously. "So what do you need from me?" she asked. "Catering for an event or something?"

Anthony nodded. "I would love that," he began. "And I would also love an endorsement from you, Meghan, as well as a small donation to my campaign."

She raised an eyebrow. "An endorsement? From *me*?"

"You're an influential person in Sandy Bay, Meghan," he told her, running a hand through his wiry auburn hair. "You're a successful business owner and you're married to a member of the police force. People in this town know you and trust you. An endorsement from you could propel my campaign forward in remarkable ways. Would you think about it?"

Just then, Trudy bustled back into the room with a cross look on her face. "What am I hearing?" she demanded, crossing her arms over her chest and glaring at Meghan and Anthony. "Meghan, you know Mayor Rose is a good friend of mine. He's been the Mayor of this town for twenty-six years. If he finds out we are supporting Anthony, it will ruin our friendship."

Anthony flashed his bright smile at Trudy. "Hey, I hear your concerns, Trudy," he began kindly, his eyes warm. "Politics can be hard. I get it. But I want to make this town a better place for everyone, and I think I can make a real impact."

Trudy narrowed her eyes. "How so?"

"I'm glad you asked," he grinned. "For starters, I want the city to fund stipends for deserving teachers. Sandy Bay teachers are the best of the best, and I want to attract and retain top talent at our local schools."

Trudy nodded. "That's nice," she agreed. "But Mayor Rose already has an incentive program for educators."

"But it doesn't include first-year teachers," Anthony added. "First-year teachers are so important, and we want to ensure every educator is compensated for their service."

Meghan smiled. "I think that's a fine idea," she commented as Trudy bit her lip. "Tell us more, Anthony. What other plans would you implement in Sandy Bay?"

"I want to start a clean energy program for the businesses in town," he told them. "Including this one. Clean energy is the future, and our local businesses need support in transitioning to clean energy models. I would love to use town funds to help businesses get the resources and materials they need to make the leap."

Trudy frowned. "That sounds too hippie-dippie for an old-fashioned gal like me," she complained.

"It would actually benefit you directly," Anthony mentioned, smiling at Trudy. "That policy would also provide a major tax credit for participating local businesses to be used in improving employee compensation."

Trudy's eyes grew large. "You're saying that if Truly Sweet starts running on clean energy, you'll give Meghan more money to pay me?"

"Exactly," Anthony nodded.

Trudy stared at him. "What about the trash at the parks? Are you going to clean up the local parks? They've been a wreck since the city cut funding for the local trash pickup. I hate seeing the parks like that, and I don't want my grand-kids to have to wade through trash when they visit me, and I take them to the park."

He reached over and placed a hand on top of hers. "Trudy, if I am elected Mayor, I will make the parks shine like they've never shined before. I'll make the parks a place you and your grandchildren can enjoy for decades to come."

"Anthony, I think you've won my vote." Trudy's lips turned upward into a smile. "These ideas will help gals like me, and I think I will be telling everyone to vote for you!"

He turned to Meghan. "And you, Meghan? Can I count on your support?"

"I'll have to think about it," she told him politely. "I want to talk with my husband about it."

"Meghan!" Trudy gasped. "You are a strong, independent woman! You don't need to ask your husband."

She shook her head. "I don't need to ask Jack, but I want to talk with him about this," she said firmly. "Anyway, Anthony, thanks for stopping by. I will be in touch."

He flashed his smile and gave a silly bow. "It was an honor," he beamed. "You ladies have a nice day."

"We will," Trudy called out as he left, and then looked at Meghan. "What's the problem?" she asked as Meghan watched Anthony leave. "He has great ideas! Having a new mayor will be like having new ideas at the bakery: hard at first, but worth it in the end. I think he will do such great things for us, and he is so handsome."

Meghan furrowed her brow. "You were the one who was so against making changes at the bakery," she countered. "And Mayor Rose is your friend. You're really going to sell him out for someone who has never been in office?"

"Anthony has great ideas," Trudy countered. "This town could use a breath of fresh air, Meghan. And maybe this bakery could, too."

That night, Meghan arrived home even more tired than the previous day. As she walked up to her front door, she willed herself to be kind and gracious to Sarah; she knew Jack liked having his mother around, and she wanted to make a good impression on her new mother-in-law.

She walked into the living room and gasped. The furniture had been rearranged; the couch, which was now covered with a chunky orange blanket, was shoved up against the back wall, new paintings hung above the fireplace, the coffee table was nowhere to be found, and the wooden bar cart that usually sat in the corner had been covered up and hidden.

"Jack?" Meghan called out. "Jack?"

"In the kitchen!"

She walked into the kitchen to find Jack seated at the kitchen table, his laptop opened to the local news station. A live video was playing, and Meghan saw Anthony waving at the camera from a podium.

"Jack, what's going on?" she asked angrily, her hands balled into fists.

"Anthony Diggs announced his mayoral campaign," he told her. "He's a great guy; we used to play on a basketball team together. Anyway, he and Mayor Rose are debating live right now. Want to watch with me?"

Before she could answer, he turned up the volume. She could hear Anthony's voice, and she slid into the chair next to her husband.

"Sandy Bay *needs* better hospitals!" Anthony declared, his face bright with excitement. "As your future Mayor, I will deliver on better healthcare for all of our citizens."

Jack stared at the screen. "He's right," he muttered as Meghan stewed silently about the furniture that had been rearranged. "We do need better hospitals."

Mayor Rose, dressed in a blue suit and green checkered tie, frowned. "The hospitals in Sandy Bay were renovated ten years ago," he argued. "Sandy Bay is a haven for families. We have great schools, thriving businesses, and low crime. Why fix what isn't broken? Sandy Bay is perfect the way it is. I don't want to take tax-payer dollars to make unnecessary changes."

Anthony shot him a look. "That kind of attitude is what will hurt this town in the long run," he stated. "Did you know we are losing the next generation, Mayor Rose? A recent study shows that eighty-six percent of Sandy Bay young adults do not return to this town after college. Think of the talent we are losing! We need to invest in technology, clean energy, and other programs and organizations that will bring our young adults back to town."

Mayor Rose raised an eyebrow. "My kids returned to this town," he said matter-of-factly. "And you did too, Mr. Diggs. I think you need to think about the claims you are making, or I'll have to put you in your place."

"My place?" Anthony laughed. "Sir, that kind of remark will put you in yours. Change and innovation are the future, and it is clear you are living in the past."

Meghan watched as Mr. Diggs eyes narrowed. "He's mad,"

she commented quietly. "Diggs is being a little arrogant, don't you think, Jack?"

Jack shrugged. "He's a good guy," he told his wife. "But Mayor Rose is a good guy, too. He stepped out of line a bit with the comment about putting Anthony in his place, but he means well. He's supportive of the police force, he's helped us double down on crime, and he makes sure we get paid what we deserve. He's done a good job, in my opinion. I think this will be a tough race."

Sarah burst into the kitchen with a grin on her face. "Meghan, I was just upstairs freshening up in my room," she began.

"My room," Meghan thought to herself, but said nothing.

"What do you think about the living room?" she chirped. "Isn't that orange blanket simply perfect? And the paintings of the cats for the fireplace? They're vintage, you know."

"It's nice," Meghan said through a forced smile. "Thank you for your help."

"It just looked too drab," Sarah sniffed. "You really need to read a few magazines or books on housekeeping and design, Meghan; every wife should know how to arrange a house in a pleasing, pretty way."

Meghan looked at her husband. "Jack," she said flatly. "What do you think of the changes to our house?"

She knew Jack could tell she was displeased, and he looked down at his feet. "I like them," he choked as Meghan gave him a swift kick under the table. "I think my mom did a great job…"

Meghan stared at him, feeling the anger rise in her chest. She could not believe her husband was not speaking up about Sarah crossing a line with the living room makeover.

"The living room is just the beginning!" Sarah squealed. "Next, I am taking over the bedroom. You will love what I do there! I'm thinking pale red walls with white trim and blue

VELVET CAKE AND MURDER

curtains. I'll do white star throw pillows for the bed, and a framed picture of the flag. It will be a patriotic theme."

Meghan frowned. If Jack didn't speak up, she was going to have to say something. She gritted her teeth and stared as Jack smiled at his mother. Her husband had clearly chosen a side, and it was not hers. Sarah Irvin had brought enough changes into their home, and now, after a long day at the bakery and discovering her home had been rearranged without her consent, Meghan was ready for a change of scenery.

4

A fter another night of horrible sleep on the living room pull out couch, Meghan was grumpy as she walked into work the next morning. With bags under her eyes and a frumpy outfit, she felt as drab as her mother-in-law must have thought her living room had previously looked.

"I have great news!" Trudy greeted her as she shuffled into the kitchen and removed her winter coat. "You won't believe this, Meghan!"

She yawned. "What's up?" she asked as she gathered her greasy hair into a ponytail. Sarah had been in the bathroom for forty-five minutes that morning, and Meghan had not been able to do her hair or brush her teeth.

"She's getting married!" Trudy grinned, and Meghan shook her head, her mind cloudy from the lack of sleep.

"Who?"

"Let me explain," Trudy began excitedly. "The first customer this morning was this real cute young gal. She looked to be about your age. She wanted a bagel with low-fat cream cheese."

Meghan sighed. "I don't get it."

"Let me finish," Trudy insisted. "She told me she wanted the low-fat cream cheese because she's getting married in four months. I asked if she booked a vendor for a cake and desserts and you know what she said?"

"Not a clue."

"She hadn't! I told her we could do a cake and matching cupcakes for her, and she was so excited about it. Her budget is *big*, Meghan; she is getting married at the art museum in Seattle, and she needs over a thousand custom cupcakes, plus a seven-tier chocolate mousse cake."

This got Meghan's attention. "Wait," her eyes widened. "You're telling me that you had a chance encounter that is going to lead to a boatload of business? Trudy, that's amazing! Way to go!"

Trudy smiled. "This is our shot, Meghan," she declared. "This will be a high-profile wedding; she said the Governor of Nebraska was invited. Think of the exposure we will get from this. We can make a powerful break into the wedding market."

Meghan gave her a hug. "Tell me everything," she said. "You said the wedding is four months away? What's the bride's name?"

Trudy bit her lip. "Ummm... I don't quite recall."

Meghan shrugged. "No worries. What about her contact information? Did you get her email or phone number?"

Her face paled. "Neither," she admitted softly. "I didn't get her contact information."

Meghan stared at her. "Well, did you give her one of our business cards?" she asked, her voice getting higher. "So she can reach out to us?"

Trudy hung her head. "I really screwed this up," she told Meghan, staring down at her brown leather loafers. "I was so excited about getting this business and breaking into the new market, and I dropped the ball."

Meghan took a deep breath. "So, you're telling me we have no way to find this woman?"

"She'll surely be back," Trudy suggested. "We had a great chat about her diet and hairdresser; she has the bangs I've always wanted to try. Anyway, it was a nice conversation. I'm sure she'll be back, Meghan."

Meghan eyed her. "I hope so," she muttered. "I could really use something going right at the moment…"

Meghan wandered into the dining room and stationed herself at the counter. The front door opened a few minutes later, and Mayor Rose walked in.

"Good morning," she greeted him, forcing herself to smile. "How is it going, Mayor Rose?"

He approached her, nodding as he walked to the counter. "I want to place a big order this morning," he informed her. "I need bagels and scones for my entire staff, as well as two-hundred mini eclairs to pass out on the street today."

She raised an eyebrow. "That *is* a big order!"

He shrugged. "As I'm sure you know, my reelection campaign has officially kicked off, and I'm hoping if I can spread a little sweetness throughout town with your treats, I can get the attention of the voters."

"Not a bad idea," she complimented him as she rang up the order. "Is that all for you today?"

He leaned in. "There is one more thing you could do for me," he asked quietly. "I've always had a lot of respect for you, Meghan. You moved to this town, opened this bakery, and have become such a respected, successful citizen of Sandy Bay."

"That is so nice of you to say," she commented pleasantly. "It feels good to be recognized for my hard work."

"It does, doesn't it? Anyway, I wanted to ask for your endorsement, Meghan. For my campaign. You and I have collaborated on several efforts over the last few years, and I think we work well together. I would like to continue that partnership in the future, and I am hoping you will openly support my campaign."

Meghan blinked. "We have worked well together," she agreed. "I have enjoyed our projects and efforts."

"Then it's settled!" he grinned. "An endorsement from you, a young, beautiful business owner, and that great husband of yours, will make for an easy campaign for me."

Meghan bit her lip. "Mayor Rose," she said softly. "I'm not quite sure…"

"About involving Jack? That's perfectly fine. You will make a wonderful spokesperson for me. Everyone loves you!"

She shook her head. "About endorsing you. I'm not sure if I will endorse anyone. It feels like a conflict of interest, and I don't know if I'm comfortable helping either of you."

The Mayor stared at her. "Meghan," he sighed. "You know me. You know my work ethic, and my commitment to this town. Diggs is a loose cannon; he is mouthy, arrogant, and too good-looking for his own good. Do you really think someone like that should be Mayor?"

She bit her lip. "I don't know," she shrugged. "But I don't think it's your place to tell me about his faults. I've told you I'm not sure, and I need you to respect that, Mayor Rose."

His face darkened. "Meghan," he said, scowling at her. "I have supported your business for years. I have made life nice and easy in Sandy Bay for the police, and that includes your husband. You can't seriously sit here and tell me that you won't endorse me. Not speaking up for me is just as bad as a vote for Diggs. I hope you realize that."

She held her head high. "I think you should leave," she said matter-of-factly. "Please."

He laughed. "Leave? I'm not done here. You and this town are gonna get swindled by this young fool with the big ego and little brain. I hope you realize what you're doing, Meghan."

She said nothing, but saw that his hands had clenched into fists. She took a step back away from him. "Please go. And I'll be canceling your order."

He shot her a nasty look and turned on his heel. As he pushed through the door, Anthony Diggs walked into the bakery.

"Figures," Mayor Rose hissed, looking back at Meghan. "I should have known he had already gotten to you, Meghan. This is rich. I give my life to this town, and this is what I get for it."

Anthony put his hands on his hips. "What's the problem?" he asked, staring at the Mayor.

"You are the problem," the mayor muttered as he stormed out of the bakery. "And the problems won't stop unless someone puts a stop to *you*."

"Everything okay?" Anthony asked as he strolled up to the counter. "What was that about?"

Meghan pursed her lips. "Same as you," she replied. "He wants my endorsement."

"What did you say?" Anthony asked.

"That is none of your business," she said cheerily. "Can I help you today?"

He nodded. "I need to order treats," he told her. "I'm hosting a town hall tonight, and I want to provide snacks for the audience. Two hundred scones and a ton of chocolate chip cookies, please."

Pamela came into the dining room. "Meghan, did I just

hear that correctly?" she asked, turning to Anthony. "That many scones? We're gonna be baking scones forever."

Anthony smiled at the teenager. "And what's your name, young lady?"

"Pamela," she replied. "And I know who you are. You're the guy who's running for mayor. My parents were talking about you this morning at breakfast."

Anthony beamed. "Wonderful," he told her. "And Pamela, what changes would you like to see in Sandy Bay? The opinions of young people are very important to me, and I would love to hear your input."

Her face brightened. "Really?"

"Really."

She thought for a moment. "Well, for starters, we need more street lights around the school and gyms," she told him. "When I work out at night or have after-school activities, I feel scared walking home in the dark."

His eyes widened. "That is very important. I will make a note of that. Anything else?"

"What about a leadership club for teenagers?" she asked. "Or an internship? It would be cool to learn more about the mayor's job and local government."

Anthony smiled. "I think that could be arranged."

"Wow, thank you for asking me," Pamela grinned. "No one has ever asked me what I want to change in our town. This is really cool."

Anthony placed a hand on her shoulder. "It was good talking with you," he nodded. "Make sure to tell your parents and any other person who is of voting age about our conversation, okay?"

"Okay!"

That evening, Meghan and Pamela drove together to the local high school where Anthony was holding the town hall meeting. It was crowded; there were people spilling out of the bleachers in the gymnasium, and Meghan could hardly hear herself over the noise of people chatting.

"This is crazy!" Pamela squealed as they navigated the crowds, pulling a wagon behind them filled with the treats Anthony had ordered. "Can you believe all of these people showed up for him? I don't blame them; he is so nice and so cute."

Meghan shrugged. She wanted to deliver the treats and leave; there was no telling what damage her mother-in-law had inflicted upon her house that day, and the last thing she wanted to do was be caught between two dueling politicians.

"There's my mom!" Pamela told Meghan, waving grandly. "And my dad."

Meghan looked over and met the eyes of Pamela's parents. She waved, and they waved back. Both were wearing pins with Anthony Diggs' face on it. "I take it you told your parents about the conversation you had with Anthony?"

"I did," Pamela grinned. "They'll definitely be voting for him now. They think it was awesome that he took the time to talk with me."

They wound their way through the aisles. "Excuse me?" Meghan asked a woman in an Anthony Diggs' shirt. She was holding a clipboard and looked very official. "Where is Anthony? I have a delivery for him."

"You'll have to wait," she told Meghan impatiently. "He's due to make his grand entrance in about a minute."

Suddenly, a piercing scream filled the gymnasium, and the room instantly went silent. "What's going on?" Pamela whispered as Meghan glanced left and right.

People were looking around, and from the back of the room, a man wearing an Anthony Diggs' button raced down the aisle and over to the woman with the clipboard.

"He's gone," the man breathed, his eyes wild with fear.

"Anthony left?" she asked in annoyance. "Why? We're supposed to start soon."

The man shook his head, and Meghan saw his eyes were filled with tears. "No," he muttered. "Anthony didn't *leave.* Anthony is DEAD!"

5

Meghan looked over at Pamela. "We have to get out of here," she told her, but amidst the chaos, she could not hear her own voice; people were screaming and darting out of their seats, and the place was in pandemonium.

Someone bumped into Meghan, and she shoved them off. The wagon carrying the treats was knocked over, and people were running over the now crushed cardboard boxes of desserts. Meghan grabbed Pamela's shoulder and held on tight.

A voice came on over the intercom. "Sandy Bay residents," it said in a panicked tone. "Please leave your things and exit the building promptly. Please exit in an orderly fash--"

The voice was cut off, and the fire alarms began ringing. Meghan let go of the wagon and threw her other arm around Pamela's body, dragging the teenager backward toward the nearest exit. People were crying and running, but Meghan worked her way through the crowd and finally, she breathed a sigh of relief as they made it outside into the chilly night air.

"What just happened?" Pamela cried in a voice that was too loud. Meghan's ears were ringing from the noise, and she imagined Pamela's were too. "Anthony's dead?"

Meghan pulled her away from the building. People were spilling out of the doors and windows, but the police had arrived and had set up barriers preventing the crowds from leaving the scene. She peered around, trying to find her husband, but she could not spot him.

"I have to find my parents," Pamela told Meghan. "Do you think they made it out okay? I tried calling them, but the cell service is terrible."

"The cell towers are probably jammed," Meghan told her. "Just stay with me for now. We'll find your family, Pamela. I promise."

"GIRLS!"

Trudy darted over to them. She was sweaty and out of breath. "Thank goodness you are both okay," she panted, leaning over and placing her hands on her knees. "That was the most I've run in twenty years."

"Are you okay?" Meghan asked, concerned as Trudy began wheezing. "This is crazy."

Trudy rose back up and gave a weak smile. "I'll be fine," she assured them. "I think I'm a little shaken up. I also forgot my purse in there… it has all of my credit cards and checks, inhaler and things. I hope no one grabs it."

"I didn't know you had asthma?"

"It hardly rears its ugly head, but sticky situations like this get me…" She held her sides and closed her eyes as she struggled to take a deep breath.

Meghan looked back at the high school. People were still exiting the building, but most had gathered in the parking lot outside. Police officers and firefighters were rushing inside.

"How about I go get your purse?" Meghan offered. "If you

can look after Pamela, I will run inside and get it. What does it look like?"

Trudy frowned, her eyebrows knitting together in a deep line. "No," she told her. "Don't go. There's a fire inside."

They could all hear the shrieks of the fire alarms, but Meghan put her hand on Trudy's shoulder and smiled. "I think someone just pulled the alarm," she informed her. "I didn't see or smell any fires. Don't you worry; I'll only be a minute. Just tell me which purse you brought."

"It's the pink and purple fake crocodile skin bag," Trudy sighed. "With the gold handles."

"That won't be easy to miss," Meghan grinned, turning to Pamela. "Stay with Trudy, okay? If your parents wander over here, go with them; otherwise, I don't want you to leave Trudy's side."

She turned on her heel and jogged over to the high school, doing her best to be surreptitious as she hovered by the back door of the gymnasium. Police officers were all over the place, but Meghan looked down at her shoes and charged inside.

The gymnasium was a total wreck; the fire alarms were still screaming, lights were flashing, and all of the chairs had been flipped over. The floor was littered with trash and personal objects, including handbags, wallets, keys, cell phones, and campaign flyers. Meghan bent down to pick up an Anthony Diggs button, studying his smiling face. Could he really be *dead*? Young, vibrant, handsome Anthony?

"Hey!" a police officer shouted at her. "Get out of here. This area is closed to the public."

Meghan bit her lip. "Sorry," she called out, quickly glancing around as she tried to spot Trudy's purse. "Just getting my bag."

"Personal items will be released to the public over the

next three weeks," she informed Meghan in a flat voice. "Please exit now, or you'll be subject to charges."

Meghan nodded, turning to leave. Her heart beat excitedly when she saw the handbag nestled beneath an overturned plastic chair as she approached the exit, and when she saw the officer's back was turned, she grabbed it, tucking it beneath her coat and hustling out of the room.

She rounded the corner to the back hallway and ran right into a tall, lithe woman with a dazed look on her face. She was dressed in an ice-blue belted coat dress that reminded Meghan of something Kate Middleton would wear. Her white-blonde hair was cut into a blunt bob that hit just below her chin, and her green eyes were filled with angst. "Sorry," she muttered as she took a step back. "I was just leaving."

Meghan pointed at the gymnasium. "You had better go fast," she warned her. "They threatened to press charges if I hung around any longer. I forgot my purse and had to run back in, and the police are trying to get everyone out of the building now."

The woman nodded. "Thanks."

Meghan saw she appeared startled, and she offered the woman her elbow.

"I'll walk with you," Meghan offered. "Come on, I know the way out."

The woman backed away into the shadows. "That's okay," she told Meghan. "Go on without me."

Meghan started to protest, but she heard footsteps approaching, and she turned to run out of the hallway and into the cold night. She saw Trudy waving at her, but before she could make it over to her, she was stopped by a pair of armed police officers.

"What were you doing in the building?" the stout male

officer questioned her. "We have been clearing the building for the last twenty minutes. What were you doing in there?"

Meghan produced the purse from beneath her coat. "My friend left her purse inside," she explained, holding up the garish bag. "She needs her bag; it has all her inhaler, credit cards and checks in it. She needs her inhaler, Officer."

"What's in the bag?" the male officer asked impatiently. "Are there any weapons or drugs in there?"

"No!" Meghan squealed. "I mean, I don't know exactly what she has in there, but I know Trudy, and I know she wouldn't carry anything she shouldn't."

The tall redheaded female officer took the bag from Meghan and opened it, rifling through it before placing it on the ground. "It's clean," she told her companion. "You're lucky there isn't anything incriminating in there, Ma'am."

"Trudy is a nice woman who just wanted her purse back," Meghan stated firmly.

"You can't just run back into a building like that," the officer scolded Meghan. "What were you thinking?"

"I don't know," Meghan blinked. "I wanted to help my friend."

The male officer studied Meghan's face. "I'm going to take your name and information," he told her. "Just in case."

Meghan gave them her name, cell phone number, and address. "Wait," the female officer stopped her. "Aren't you Jack Irvin's wife?"

"I am," Meghan confirmed. "I'm Jack Irvin's wife, Meghan."

"Let her go," the female officer instructed the male officer. "Sorry to hold you up, Mrs. Irvin," she apologized to Meghan. "Standard protocol for situations like this. I hope you understand."

Meghan smiled. "I get it," she told them. "I'll just be going, now..."

She walked away quickly, but before she could reach her friends, she saw the woman in the blue coat dress out of the corner of her eye. The woman looked lost, and Meghan hurried over to her. "Hey," she greeted. "Are you okay? I'm glad you got out of there. Did the police question you, too?"

The woman's lips trembled. "They did," she agreed, hanging her head.

"Do you need me to call someone?" Meghan asked her, putting a hand on her shoulder. "You don't look like you're doing okay. They have ambulances over there, you know. I could go get a medic for you."

The woman looked up at Meghan, her green eyes large. "That's okay," she insisted. "I'm fine."

Meghan squeezed her shoulder. "I don't think we've met," she told her. "I'm Meghan Irvin. I own the bakery in town. What's your name?"

The woman blinked. "I'm Bonnie," she murmured, tucking a loose lock of blonde hair behind her ears. Meghan saw a giant glittering emerald cut wedding ring on her left hand as she moved the hair. "Bonnie Diggs."

"Wait," Meghan's jaw dropped. "Bonnie Diggs? So, you're…"

"Yes," Bonnie pursed her lips. "That's right. I'm Anthony Diggs' wife."

6

Meghan snuggled beneath the thick down comforter, her eyes still closed as she wiggled her toes and settled into a comfortable position. It was her day off, and after a long, stressful week, along with the craziness from the disastrous town hall the night before, she was eager to spend a long morning resting on her pull out couch bed.

Siesta snuggled closer to her, licking her ear. She pulled the small dog into her arms, enjoying the warmth she provided as they cuddled together. Jack had had to leave early that morning to go to the station, but with all three dogs piled in bed with her, Meghan was content.

"Nothing could ruin this cozy morning," she thought to herself as Fiesta burrowed between her legs.

"GOOD MORNING!"

She stifled a groan as Sarah barreled into the living room and flicked on all the lights. "Meghan, wake up! We have a lot to do today, Mrs. Lazy! Come on. The early bird gets the worm."

Meghan clung to the blankets, shaking her head. "It's my

day off, Sarah," she protested. "And it's been a long week. I really need to catch up on my sleep."

Sarah sprung over to the couch and pulled the down comforter off of her. Meghan opened her eyes. Sarah's blonde hair was pulled into a French braid, and she wore a burgundy turtleneck and black slacks. Her blue eyes were bright with excitement, and she perched herself on the corner of the couch.

"Days off are the best days for running errands," she informed Meghan, her smile wide. "Don't you want to have everything you need to make dinner tonight?"

"It's Jack's turn to make dinner tonight," Meghan told her. "Not mine."

Sarah frowned. "A wife should always be ready to make a nice dinner for her husband," she corrected her. "Jack's father and I don't take turns making dinner. It's my job to make meals for him. That's what being a wife is all about."

Meghan vehemently disagreed; being a wife was about partnership, respect, and sharing, and that included sharing the chores and household responsibilities. Before she could reply to Sarah, her mother-in-law stood up and tapped her wristwatch. "We're leaving in fifteen minutes," she told Meghan. "Scoot! You can't go to the market dressed like that."

Fifteen minutes later, Meghan felt sullen as she and Sarah drove to the market. Meghan had hurriedly thrown on a casual outfit of opaque black leggings, a baggy rust red sweatshirt, and Ugg boots, and Sarah had scowled at her outfit. "Are we going to the gym?" she asked in a sickly-sweet tone. "Or to run errands?"

"Errands," Meghan replied flatly.

"Then why are you dressed as though you are off to the gym? I never dressed like a gym rat when I was your age. I don't see how that's good for your reputation, either.

Meghan Irvin, businesswoman and wife, skulking around town in leggings? It just isn't a good look, Meghan. Maybe for a supermodel, but we both know you aren't that tiny!"

Meghan stared at Sarah. Everything that came out of her mouth was always in a polite, loving tone, but the sting of her words was hard to miss. "My outfit is fine," she replied firmly.

They arrived at the market, and Meghan noticed the store, usually quiet and relaxed, was abuzz. Shoppers were stopped along the perimeter of the aisles, frantically chatting with each other, and the sounds of whispers sounded like the frenetic buzzing of a beehive.

"What's going on?" Sarah asked as she got a cart and walked down the produce aisle. "What is everyone talking about?"

Meghan pointed at the display of local newspapers. "A local politician was killed last night," she explained quietly as they walked. "He was running for Mayor of Sandy Bay, and according to the newspaper, he was strangled right before he was set to speak at a local town hall."

Sarah's eyes grew large. "That's terrible," she choked. "Sandy Bay was never this unsafe when Jack's father and I lived here. Maybe you two should move in with us. I don't want my grandchildren living in this sort of seedy place."

Meghan rolled her eyes. Giving Sarah grandchildren was not on the agenda for at least another two years, and she had already explained that to her mother-in-law.

"Why don't I grab the vegan cheese?" Meghan asked. "You can get the vegetables."

Sarah laughed. "Vegan cheese? For who? Don't tell me you're some sort of hippie now, Meghan."

She shook her head. "It's for your son," she smiled, trying not to gloat. "He can't eat cheese."

Sarah peered at her curiously. "Honey," she smirked. "We

Irvins originated in Sweden. Cheese is a way of life for us. My Jacky loves cheese! You must be mistaken. Surely you should know the things your husband prefers and doesn't like, no?"

She shrugged. "Over the holidays, Jack was having a bellyache. The doctor told us that he is lactose intolerant. No more cheese."

Sarah narrowed her eyes. "My son? No. We Irvins have stomachs of steel. The doctor must be mistaken. Let me guess, did you drag him to some holistic doctor or a therapist or something? Those people are total crocks."

"Dr. Tanzel earned her MD from Harvard," Meghan informed her. "I think she's right, too; Jack's bellyaches stopped when we cut out dairy, and his skin and energy levels have been better, too."

Sarah said nothing, and Meghan quickly walked away from her. She was irritated that her mother-in-law thought she knew *everything* about *her* husband. Sarah may have raised Jack, but Meghan was his *wife*. Surely, she knew a little more about the man than his mother, who lived several hours away, did.

She rounded the corner and entered the health food aisle. She scanned the shelves, trying to find the brand of vegan cheese she and Jack both liked. As she wandered, she over-heard two women, both young and pretty, nearby whispering to each other, both leaning over their carts, their heads close together.

"What a shame that he's gone," the skinny brunette said, licking her lips. "I thought I would be Mrs. Diggs someday. I always thought that he and Bonnie wouldn't last; he was so outgoing, and she is so...plain."

The other woman, a busty woman with hip-length raven hair, shook her head. "Bonnie isn't plain," she argued. "I think she's gorgeous. Those cheekbones and her hair? She's a classic beauty. She's just quiet. And she's never around; I never saw them together, and rumor is that she spends most weekends off in California with her parents. She doesn't even like Sandy Bay."

"Quiet or stuck up?" the brunette asked sarcastically. "And that hair and those cheekbones? I heard Anthony bought her good looks for her. Don't you remember her in high school? She was nothing to look at."

"But Anthony was," the dark-haired woman smiled dreamily. "That smile and those dimples! He always made me swoon."

Meghan wondered about Bonnie Diggs. She had seemed so shaken up after the town hall, and it felt wrong that these women were judging the new widow.

"Did they date in high school?" she heard the brunette ask. "I don't remember Anthony and Bonnie hanging around together."

The dark-haired woman shook her head. "He was all wrapped up with that other girl...what was her name? She was a freshman when we were seniors. I think she still lives in town!"

"I don't remember," her friend commented. "But I wish he had been dating me!"

"Such a tragedy that he's gone," the other woman sighed sadly. "What a loss of a gorgeous man."

They noticed Meghan staring, and she quickly grabbed a block of vegan cheese and hurried back to her mother-in-law. "There you are," Sarah said as she returned. "You were gone forever, Meghan. It's quite rude to leave people waiting for you like that."

As they drove home, Sarah could not stop complaining; she complained about the selection at the market, she complained about the traffic downtown, she complained about the snow falling and the weather, and she complained about Meghan's bakery.

"Jack says you're planning to break into the wedding market?" Sarah asked as they drove past Truly Sweet. "Honestly, Meghan, that's a lot of work for you to do. Do you really think it's a good idea to add more to your plate? How will Jack feel if you are never home?"

Meghan bit her lip. "We haven't really made a decision about breaking into the wedding market," she told her mother-in-law. "But I think it would be a great opportunity for my business, and for my family. Jack and I could do so much with the extra income."

Sarah raised an eyebrow. "Life isn't all about money," she countered. "It's about family and making your husband happy. Besides, Jack tells me you have a good thing going at the bakery now. Why change it? Too much change is never a good thing, Meghan."

"Like the way you changed my living room?" Meghan thought to herself. "Is she hearing herself? Could she *be* any more of a meddling mother-in-law?"

She did the math in her head and realized that Sarah's stay was not even close to over. How was she going to survive another few weeks with her mother-in-law? Sarah had taken over her bedroom, her bathroom, and now, she was trying to take over the bakery. Meghan could not take much more; it was time to talk to her husband about his mother.

When they arrived home, Dash, Fiesta, and Siesta greeted them at the front door. "Hi, babies," Meghan happily greeted them as she balanced the bags of groceries. "Back up, Dash. Mommy is trying to get in."

Sarah wrinkled her nose. "Dogs should not be allowed in the house," she declared as she stuck up her nose at Siesta, who was licking her ankle. "They are filthy creatures. My cats don't bring in dirt like these three do. I can't believe Jack allows you to have three dogs."

Meghan stared at her. "Dash was *Jack's* to start with," she informed her. "I brought Fiesta and Siesta into the equation. Jack had Dash for years before we even met."

"Still," Sarah continued. "Dogs don't belong inside. You should get cats instead. Jack grew up with cats, and we have cats at home. Whenever those dogs pass away, you should get cats. Jack would love a house filled with cats!"

Meghan could not take it any longer. "The dogs stay in the house," she stated, her head held high. "They're my babies, and they belong inside of *my* house."

She silently put the groceries away as quickly as she could, and then she rounded up the three dogs. She put their leashes and harnesses on, and took off, going for a walk to clear her head.

Meghan took the dogs down the street and over to the beach, her favorite place to spend time with them. It was an unusually sunny day, and she smiled as the warm rays of sun kissed her cheeks. The beach was covered with a light layer of snow, and she let the dogs off their leashes. They ran wildly through the icy water, splashing and playing as they barked joyfully.

The beach was empty except for two figures in the distance. Meghan squinted her eyes. She could make out the figures of a man and a woman, and from their body language, it looked like they were arguing. The man was waving his hands erratically, and the woman's hands were on her hips. She was shaking her head.

"That's how I want to respond to Sarah," she laughed to herself as she saw the woman pumping her fists in the air. "I want to give her a piece of my mind."

As the pair walked closer to her, Meghan was shocked to see the man was Mayor Rose. She didn't recognize the woman, and as soon as Mayor Rose made eye contact with Meghan, he pulled the woman away by the elbow.

"That wasn't Mrs. Rose," she said aloud as the dogs kept barking.

She watched as the mayor hurried away with the mystery woman. Who was he fighting with? What were they fighting about? Meghan did not know, but she had a bad feeling deep in her gut that something was amiss.

7

"So who did it?" Pamela asked as she, Trudy, and Meghan huddled around a table at the bakery the next morning. "Meghan, do you know anything? Has Jack mentioned it to you? He's been assigned to the case, right?"

Meghan took a sip of her green tea and shook her head. "You know he can't say anything to me about his cases," she reminded them. "It's unprofessional."

Pamela rolled her eyes. "You would think the wife of the town detective would have the scoop on everything," she complained. "You never know anything."

Trudy swatted Pamela on the wrist. "Don't be rude," she admonished the teenager. "Meghan is under a lot of stress right now. Her mother-in-law is staying at her house for several weeks."

Pamela raised an eyebrow. "So? I don't get it. I always love my boyfriends' moms."

Trudy laughed. "Trust me. You'll understand when you're older."

Pamela crossed her arms. "I just want to know who did

it," she pouted. "Anthony was so handsome and nice. I think stuffy old Mayor Rose did it."

Trudy bit her lip. "I don't know if you're wrong," she sighed. "Roland *was* known for his temper back in school; he once beat up a guy on another basketball team just for looking at him the wrong way."

Meghan held up her hands. "Whoa," she stopped them. "Whoa. Wasn't that like... thirty years ago? It doesn't seem fair to bring up someone's high school mistakes when talking about a *murder*."

Trudy stared at her. "You told us you saw him on the beach with a mystery woman yesterday," she said pointedly. "Clearly Mayor Rose has some dirty little secrets. Maybe this is one of them."

Pamela shrugged. "A murder is a pretty big secret," she breathed. "Anthony *was* younger, better looking, and more articulate. I think he would have won the election, and I think Mayor Rose killed him before Anthony could take his job."

Meghan looked between them. "You really think Mayor Rose, a lifelong member of this community, someone we all know, would be so bold as to kill a political rival? It's the Sandy Bay mayoral election, not the United States Presidency!"

Trudy furrowed her brow. "People can do strange things when they feel threatened," she told them. "Mayor Rose ran this town for nearly thirty years. He had a lot to lose. Maybe he just cracked."

Meghan cocked her head to the side in disbelief. "I don't know," she added. "I just think it sounds a bit ridiculous. I don't think getting into a fistfight in high school means someone has the capacity to kill. Don't you think that sounds extreme?"

Pamela's eyes widened. "Maybe. Or Maybe not."

Meghan sighed. "I wonder what Jack knows," she wondered aloud. "He hasn't mentioned anything about it…"

Trudy smiled. "He's probably too busy reliving his childhood as a mama's boy," she joked, though Meghan did not laugh. "Has she rearranged your house any further? I'm surprised she hasn't thrown out all your clothes or tried to take your dogs to the pound. That woman really sounds like a piece of work."

Meghan groaned. "This morning, she started in on my hair," she lamented as she buried her face in her hands. "Meghan? That wavy look is so untidy. Why don't you try my curling iron or better yet, a straightener? Clean up those waves for good?"

"She did not say that to you," Pamela gasped. "Meghan! Your hair is pretty. It's so healthy and shiny."

Meghan tossed her long, wavy hair behind her shoulder. "I used to straighten it every single day in high school," she explained as she grabbed a lock and played with it between her thumb and pointer finger. "All the other girls at school had straight blonde or strawberry blonde hair, and I had this mess of wavy dark hair. I was so self-conscious about it, too. I started straightening it every day, but by the time I went away to college, I had damaged my hair. I had to cut it all off into a dreadful pixie cut and start from scratch."

Pamela's eyes grew large with curiosity. "You had a pixie cut?" she squealed. "I can't even imagine!"

"It looked awful on me," Meghan told her. "Awful. But it grew back, and I haven't straightened it since. I like my natural hair. It's who I am."

Trudy scowled. "That lady needs to back off," she hissed. "Imagine if your children have your hair and she says nasty things to them about it. Then what?"

"Then she'll have to deal with *me*," Meghan replied evenly.

Later that afternoon, Meghan and Pamela were frosting a batch of red velvet cupcakes when they heard Trudy moan. "We're out of eggs," she called out from the back of the kitchen. "Meghan? How did this happen?"

Meghan went to the walk-in refrigerator and frowned as she surveyed the empty shelf where the eggs were supposed to be. "Trudy? Did you forget to order them?" she asked, confused by the mistake.

"It was Pamela's job," Trudy told her quietly. "Remember when we talked about her doing more administrative and managerial work in the new year? I assigned her to do inventory and the groceries this week, and…."

Meghan turned to look at Pamela. The teenager was happily spreading bright scarlet icing across a red velvet cupcake, a smile on her face as she moved her hands in a rhythmic way. "Maybe she should just stick to baking," Meghan suggested softly as they stood in the refrigerator. "Maybe managing just isn't her stuff."

Trudy shook her head. "Every woman needs to know how to manage, plan, and organize," she insisted. "Pamela needs to know these things; we don't want to just relegate her to baking. What about when she buys a house, or does her taxes? If she doesn't learn this stuff, she'll be reliant on someone else. That isn't what I want for her…"

"You're right," Meghan agreed. "She has to learn. I'll sit down with her later and talk about it. We can teach her some better strategies. For now, though, we desperately need eggs. And a lot of them…"

"Let's head to the market," Trudy said. "Pamela can hold down the fort, and we'll run over and get the eggs."

Fifteen minutes later, Meghan and Trudy arrived at the market. Each fetched a shopping cart; they needed at least fifty cartons of eggs, and Meghan wasn't even sure if her car would hold everything they needed.

She saw the newspaper stand and frowned as she spotted a large photo of Anthony's face on the front page. The atmosphere in the store was similar to when she had been there with Sarah; the place was abuzz with frantic whispering, and Trudy looked at Meghan in confusion as they wandered the aisles. "What is going on here?"

"I think it's about Anthony," Meghan told her softly. "Apparently he had a cult-like following in town. I had no idea…"

Trudy wrinkled her nose. "People can get so crazy over a good-looking, well-spoken man. It's embarrassing," she declared, holding her head high as they approached the dairy aisle.

There were two women huddled near the eggs. "Excuse me?" Meghan said politely, but they did not hear her. They were feverishly whispering, and Meghan craned her neck to hear them.

"And his voice. That smooth, buttery voice. It just sent me over the edge. When I would watch his television ads or campaign speeches, it made my heart flutter."

Meghan turned to Trudy and scowled. "Isn't that gross?" she sighed. "Carrying on like that over a man who is dead? And a married man, at that? If ladies made over Jack like that, I would be sick, especially if he were *dead*."

"His face was like a movie star's," the woman's friend cooed. "Can I tell you a secret? I had a news clipping about him tucked into the drawer in my nightstand. Sometimes, I would take it out just to look at his gorgeous face."

"If your husband knew, he would just die!" the other woman giggled.

"But now, Anthony's dead, and there's no one cute around town," her friend complained.

Meghan turned to Trudy, disgusted by the conversation, but she realized her friend was quickly walking away.

"Trudy?" she called out, confused by her exit. "Trudy? Where are you going?"

She turned on her heel, abandoning her cart. Where was Trudy going? Why had she left so quickly? Was Trudy hiding something from her, or worse, did Trudy know something about *Anthony*?

8

Meghan followed Trudy down the aisle and was relieved to find her. Trudy was chatting with a woman she didn't recognize, a pretty brunette with sharp features and spiral curls that fell to her shoulders.

"Hey," she greeted them. "Trudy? Are you okay?"

Trudy turned to her. "I was just apologizing to Erin," she explained. "I am so, so sorry."

Erin, the brunette, shook her head. "No, Trudy," she protested. "I am sorry. You have no idea how sorry I am."

Trudy waved her hands. "You couldn't possibly be more sorry than I am. I am just so sorry, Erin."

Meghan cleared her throat. "What's going on, ladies?"

Trudy smiled at Erin. "This is Erin Rogers! She is the woman who popped by the bakery the other day. She wants us to make her wedding treats. I forgot to get her contact information, and as we were shopping, I spotted her. I had to run over and apologize for not reaching out about the cakes. Erin, I am so glad I found you!"

Erin nodded graciously. "It's my fault," she protested. "I

should have left you my business card or tried to find you online."

Meghan reached out her hand. "Erin, I'm Meghan Irvin, the owner of the bakery. It's a pleasure to meet you. Congratulations on your engagement!"

Erin grinned. "Thank you. I couldn't be happier to meet you, Meghan. What a pleasure."

Meghan studied Erin's face. She appeared to be a few years older than Meghan, but with her flawless skin and lovely figure, Meghan imagined she would make a beautiful bride.

"I just got married," she shared with Erin. "A few months ago. Being a newlywed is such a treat, but I remember how fun it was to be engaged."

Erin grinned, holding up her left hand and flashing her engagement ring at them. It was a round cut diamond with a delicate halo of tiny diamonds and a silver band, and Meghan clapped her hands eagerly at the sight of it. "I love the halo," she complimented as Erin wiggled her fingers playfully. "It's so unique."

"It's exactly what I wanted," Erin shared, reaching over to give the large round diamond a gentle stroke. "My love picked it out without any help, and he did so well. He knew exactly what I wanted. I didn't even have to hint."

"It sounds like you two are a match made in Heaven," Trudy sighed happily. "You'll be such a gorgeous bride. Do you have a dress picked out?"

Erin pulled out her phone. "Do you want to see a photo?"

"Yes!" Meghan and Trudy cried.

Erin scrolled through her photos and found a picture of herself standing on a pedestal at a bridal boutique. "Ta da!"

"Wow," Meghan smiled excitedly. "What is that fabric called? I love it!"

"Is it satin?" Trudy asked.

"It's charmeuse," Erin explained. "It's like satin but a bit lighter."

"The cowl neck is dreamy," Meghan told her. "And your figure is to die for!"

"My fiance is expecting me to be in a big poofy dress," she grinned giddily. "The form-fitting dress will be such a shock to him. I think he will like it, though. Let's face it, girls: I'll never be this skinny again! I've been on a wedding diet for the last three months, and after we say I DO, I want to chow down!"

"That's the perfect segue into talking about partnering with the bakery," Meghan told her.

"What are your thoughts about the wedding cakes and treats?" she asked eagerly. "Trudy mentioned it was a big wedding? Are you thinking just cakes, or should we incorporate other treats?"

Erin licked her lips. "You're making me hungry. I want something simple; a nice carrot cake or German chocolate cake would be my preference, but James, my darling fiance, wants something a little more daring."

"Do you know what he has in mind?" Meghan asked. "We could do something unique, like a chocolate fountain? Or something simple, like a variety of cakes."

"He loves red velvet cake," Erin shared with them. "It's his favorite. He hasn't had a lot of opinions about this wedding, but just last night, he told me he wants a red velvet cake with ten tiers. *Ten*! Can you imagine?"

Trudy beamed. "Red velvet cakes are some of our favorites," she assured the bride-to-be. "And we can easily do ten tiers. Do you have any more requests?"

Erin pursed her lips. "Could we do some German chocolate cupcakes as a little compromise? That way I get what I want, and he gets what he wants?"

"I love it!" Meghan exclaimed. "Here, let me give you my

card. We can do a tasting when you are ready, and if we are a good fit, I'll draw up a contract."

Erin took the card and put it in her purse. "It was so great running into you both," she smiled. "What a lucky day this is."

"It was fate," Meghan said. "Erin, it was so nice to meet you."

"And you," Erin told her. "I will certainly be in touch."

Trudy and Meghan watched as she walked away. "That was great," Meghan told her. "I can't believe you found her, Trudy. That will be some great business for us."

"I think your instincts about the wedding market are good," Meghan praised her. "I'm so glad you ran up to her, Trudy. Great job!"

Trudy grinned. "Wasn't she lovely?" she asked. "I think she will be really fun to partner with, too."

"I agree," Meghan told her.

Trudy looked down at her black snow boots. "Thanks for helping seal the deal," she sighed as Meghan raised an eyebrow. "I was just so excited about the business when I met her, and it was easy to forget about the steps to close a deal. It's one thing to have a customer have interest, but it's another to get them in the door for a tasting, signing contracts, and everything else."

Meghan shook her head. "It's one of my strengths," she explained kindly. "Just like managing the bakery is yours. We're a great team, Trudy. You run the bakery like a champ, I do operations well, and Pamela has a gift for baking. Without one of us, it wouldn't work the same way. We are so lucky to have each other."

Trudy's eyes shined. "We really are, aren't we?"

On their way out of the market, after loading up the car and deciding to walk to grab a quick cup of coffee, they stopped to admire a performer who was juggling on the town square.

"Look at him go!" Trudy laughed as he spun the glittering balls over his head. "We need him in the bakery; can you imagine how fast we could make crepes if we had someone with those fast hands in our kitchen?"

Meghan chuckled, imagining the performer flipping crepes at the speed he was juggling the balls. "Maybe we can add him to the team," she joked.

It was a cold day; giant snowflakes were falling gracelessly to the ground, and Meghan's hair was soaking wet as the wet flakes clung to her. "Are you ready to go?" she asked Trudy after a few more minutes. "That cup of coffee is screaming my name!"

"Let's go," Trudy agreed, and they turned to make their way to the coffee shop. "Actually, I'm going to run back into the market to use the bathroom. Be right back!"

As Trudy left, Meghan heard someone groan. She looked down and realized she was standing on someone's foot.

"Sorry!" she cried, removing her foot from the taupe leather boot she had been crushing. "So sorry!"

She glanced up to see the boot belonged to Bonnie Diggs. "Bonnie," she whispered. "I am so sorry, Bonnie. I really should have watched where I was going."

Bonnie's face was dark. Dressed in a red wool coat dress and matching gloves, she looked angry as she stared at Meghan.

"I hope I didn't upset her," Meghan thought to herself as she tried to muster a better apology for Bonnie. "She looks like she's ready to *kill* me."

9

"You're making quite a habit of stepping on my toes," Bonnie commented as Meghan took a step back from her.

"I am so sorry," she apologized as she nervously tucked her hair behind her ears. "I didn't see you there, Bonnie."

"Clearly," Bonnie replied flatly.

"I hope I didn't ruin your boots," Meghan bit her lip, looking down to see a large brown scuff on the shoe she had stepped on.

"It's fine," Bonnie sighed. "These were a gift from my husband, but they were getting old. I was going to throw them out soon anyway."

Meghan stared at her. Bonnie's white blonde hair was swept back into a French twist, and with her beautiful coat and matching gloves, she epitomized elegance.

"How are you doing?" Meghan asked her quietly. "I imagine this must be a very difficult time for you."

Bonnie shrugged. "That's what everyone's been asking me," she replied. "In all honesty, Anthony wasn't around a lot at home," she admitted softly. "He was always working or traveling for business with his business partner, or at the gym. I spent a lot of time by myself here. I started spending more time with my parents at their home in Arcata. It was better than being alone in this town...."

Meghan felt her heart sink. Bonnie's voice was tinged with so much sadness. "Didn't you grow up here?"

Bonnie nodded. "I did," she confirmed. "But my parents moved to California when I graduated high school. Most of my friends from childhood have left town, too. All I had left here was Anthony. Now, I don't know what I'm going to do..."

Bonnie's chin began to tremble.

"I'm really sorry," Meghan told her again. "I know what it's like to be somewhere and feel alone. I moved here only knowing one person, and it was quite difficult. If you ever need to talk...well...my door is always open."

Bonnie smiled. "That's very kind of you," she replied. "Say, did you know my husband well? You look to be around my age..."

"I didn't," Meghan told her. "Just in passing, really."

"Good," Bonnie said curtly. "I'm glad to hear it."

Meghan watched in confusion as Bonnie turned on her heel and strode away, the tail of her coat flapping in the wind. "That was an odd question to ask," she thought as Bonnie turned the corner and out of her sight. "I wonder what that was all about..."

Trudy reappeared from the market. "All done," she told Meghan. "What's with the sour look on your face?"

"It's nothing," Meghan lied, still puzzled about her interaction with Bonnie. "Nothing at all."

After grabbing coffee, they drove back to the bakery, careful to avoid patches of ice on the roads. Meghan stared out the window, still pondering what Bonnie had said.

"What are you thinking about?" Trudy asked. "You've

been quiet since I got back from the bathroom, Meghan. What's wrong?"

Meghan wrinkled her nose. "What do you know about Bonnie Diggs?"

"Bonnie Diggs?" Trudy wondered. "What's got you thinking about Bonnie Diggs?"

Meghan crossed her arms over her chest. "I ran into her today when you went to the bathroom," she explained. "Like, literally ran into her. I accidentally stepped on her foot."

Trudy laughed. "You're a little clumsy, Meghan.'"

"She seems a little...off," Meghan continued. "What do you know about her?"

Trudy thought for a moment. "She was a few years younger than Anthony," she began. "Closer to your age, really. She went to college in Paris, France, and even modeled in Paris for a few years. Anthony didn't have any interest in her in high school, but when she came home for Christmas at the height of her modeling career, he swept her off her feet. They were married within the year."

"Wow!" Meghan's eyes widened. "No wonder she is so elegant. A model in Paris!"

"She's a classy lady," Trudy told her. "As I'm sure you realized."

"She seems so...disconnected from Anthony," Meghan observed as she thought of her encounters with Bonnie. "She is so different than any other grieving widow I've met."

Trudy shrugged. "People grieve differently," she countered. "Besides, Bonnie has been through a lot in the last few years. I'm sure she's accustomed to grieving..."

Meghan's jaw dropped. "Accustomed to *grieving?* What do you mean?"

"Her twins," Trudy murmured. "She and Anthony were going to have twins. Five years ago, she was pregnant with twins. She was the cutest pregnant woman; her stomach was so round, but with her little figure, it looked like she had a beach ball beneath her dresses. She was cute as a button."

"What happened?" Meghan whispered. "To the twins?"

Trudy's face fell. "It was a horrible accident," she muttered as they turned onto the street and pulled up to the bakery. "Anthony was driving, and there was a terrible accident. She lost the babies and nearly died herself."

Meghan breathed in sharply. "How terrible," she moaned. "Poor Anthony. Poor Bonnie. Her heart must have been broken."

Trudy shook her head. "Something broke in Bonnie that day," she commented as they got out of the car and opened the trunk. "She's never been the same."

Meghan was shaken, and as they walked into the bakery, both carrying bags of eggs, she could not get Bonnie off her mind. What must it have been like to lose her children, and now, her husband? Bonnie certainly needed a friend, and Meghan was determined to show her kindness.

"Pamela, we need your help," Trudy called out as they walked into the dining room. "Can you please give us a hand?"

Pamela ran into the dining room with a funny look on her face. "What's wrong?" Meghan asked. "Are you okay?"

Pamela shook her head, her eyes large and her mouth in a thin line. "It's not okay," she whispered. "We have a major problem, Meghan. A MAJOR problem."

Just then, a familiar figure strode out of the kitchen and into the dining room. It was Sarah Irvin, dressed in one of the bakery's signature yellow aprons. "It's about time you got back," she told Meghan as Meghan's mouth fell open. "I've been waiting for you! We have a lot to do around here, ladies!"

10

M eghan stared at her mother-in-law. What was Sarah Irvin doing at *her* bakery? Meghan had not invited her. Did she really think she was going to take over Meghan's house *and* job?

"What's that face for?" Sarah asked, placing her hands on her hips. "You look as though you aren't happy to see your mother-in-law, Miss Meghan!"

Meghan pasted a smile on her face. "I'm always happy to see you, Sarah," she replied. "I just wasn't expecting you here today."

"It's a surprise!" she told her. "Jack suggested it. He thought I would have such a great time helping you around the bakery, and I decided to swing by. What's on our agenda for today? Pamela told me we need to make some batches of raisin cookies and fruit tarts, but I have some better ideas."

"Better ideas?" Meghan asked.

"First, we should start with the dining room," Sarah told them, raising her hands and spinning around in a dramatic circle. "It's a bit filthy in here, don't you think? There is dust everywhere. You can't think it's okay to let your guests eat in a place this messy, can you?"

Meghan bit her lip. "We wiped down everything this morning," she explained, trying her best to be patient. "Things get messy throughout the day. We give it all a good scrubbing at the end of the night, Sarah. That's our standard procedure, and it's worked well for us for the last few years."

Sarah sniffed. "I just don't think it's appropriate to let guests eat with dust bunnies in sight, but if that's the way you like it, fine. I guess that explains the dust in the corners at your home, doesn't it?"

Meghan could feel Trudy and Pamela's eyes on her. "Trudy, why don't you give Sarah some things to do?" she asked. "Pamela, you can help me unload these eggs."

They walked outside in silence, and once they had exited the bakery, Pamela turned to Meghan and squealed. "She is terrible!"

"She's a little much, isn't she?" Meghan frowned.

"None of my boyfriends have ever had moms like her," Pamela declared. "How did you end up with such a crazy one?"

Meghan closed her eyes. "It's a bit different to be married to someone," she explained to the teenager.

"How?" Pamela asked.

"I'm not sure how to explain it," Meghan told her. "But it's different. You'll understand someday."

Pamela turned up her nose. "I hope not," she stated. "I hope I *never* have a mother-in-law like yours."

After they brought the eggs inside, Meghan snuck into the bathroom with her cell phone.

Your mother is here. Why did you send her over here without telling me? She's getting in the way, Jack.

She finished the text to her husband, her heart pounding. Had Jack really thought it was a good idea to send his mother to her for the entire day?

Her phone buzzed, and she glanced down at the new text from her husband.

I am so sorry. I will take care of it. I love you. XO

"He had better take care of it," she thought to herself as she returned to the dining room to find her mother-in-law ordering Pamela about.

An hour later, Jack walked through the front door of the bakery with a cautious smile on his face. He was dressed in his work uniform, with his collared navy blue shirt, matching blue trousers, and official pins.

"He knows he's good looking," Meghan grumbled to herself as her husband flashed her a bright smile. "But good looks aren't gonna make up for this."

"My baby!" Sarah shrieked as she dropped the broom she was holding and dashed over to her son. "What are you doing here, honey?"

"I'm here to take my favorite lady to lunch," he told her as he stared at Meghan.

"Well, isn't that sweet?" Sarah gushed. "I hope Meghan will let me take an hour or two to go to lunch with you. She runs a tight ship around here, Jack. I didn't realize she was so demanding."

Jack cleared his throat. "I actually came to take my wife out to lunch," he told her. "Meghan? Can you spare an hour or two for your husband?"

Meghan nodded. "I think I can make it work."

She turned to Trudy. "Can you hold down the fort while I am gone?"

Before Trudy could answer, Sarah jumped in. "I will keep

things running for you, Meghan," she assured her daughter-in-law. "Don't you worry about a thing. In fact, when you return, I bet things around here will be even *better* than when you left."

Meghan fetched her coat and gloves and left the bakery with her husband. "Where do you want to go?" Jack asked as they walked down the street.

"Anywhere," Meghan muttered. "Anywhere but here."

Jack turned to stare at her, his blue eyes filled with concern. "She's really gotten to you, hasn't she?"

Meghan stopped and faced her husband. "Jack, she criticizes *everything* I do," she began, balling her hands in frustration. "She always has something bad to say about the way I keep our house, or the way I dress... it's getting on my nerves."

"I'm sorry, babe," he said earnestly, putting his hands on her shoulders.

"You don't seem too sorry," she shot back. "You never step in. I expect my husband to stand up for me, and you just let her walk all over me. It isn't okay, Jack."

He took a deep breath and exhaled. "What can I do?"

She looked left and then right. "Let's go grab a bite to eat," she said quietly. "I don't want the entire town to hear about this."

They walked to Keagan's Vegan, the trendy vegan restaurant in town. They were seated at a high-top table set for two. Meghan admired the shelf of succulents and amaryllis above the table. She loved the aesthetic of Keagan's; with the exposed brick walls, whitewashed wooden floors, and abundance of plants and greenery, it was a nice escape from the dreary winter landscape.

"Get anything you'd like," Jack urged her. "It's my treat."

"I think I need a drink," she scoffed as she perused the menu. "See? Your mother has driven me to drinking, Jack."

"That isn't funny," he told her.

She sat up straight and folded her hands primly on the table. "I need to know you are on my side, Jack."

He nodded. "I am on your side," he promised her. "I should have been speaking up more with my mom. I'm sorry I let you down."

A waitress appeared with two menus and a tray of waters. She placed everything on the table in front of them. "Here you go," she smiled. "What can I get started for you today?"

"I want the mushroom burger with cashew cheese," Meghan told her. "And a side of sweet potato fries."

"I'll have the same," Jack followed. "Please."

She grinned. "The sweet potato fries are the best," she praised. "I'll have that right in for you two."

Meghan watched as the waitress walked away and then turned back to her husband. "So what are we going to do?" she asked. "Your mother is here, and I want to make sure I survive the next few weeks."

Jack reached for her hands. "That's all I want."

"I need to know you are on my side," she explained to him.

"I'm always on your side," he insisted. "Look, Meghan, I know my mother can be a lot to take; she has a huge personality, and she likes things done a certain way. That said, YOU are my wife, my partner, and the lady of the house. YOU are in charge, Meghan, not her. I am going to do a better job of speaking up when she is out of line."

"Okay," she sighed.

He shook his head. "I should have set better boundaries with her early on," he told his wife. "I should have stepped in. I'm sorry I didn't stand up for you, and that you are so frustrated. I can only imagine how hard this has been for you."

Meghan's heart began to warm. Jack was on *her* side; she had been worried that he wouldn't believe her, or that he would put her down for her feelings toward his mother, but he was telling her everything she needed to hear. She was pleased, and she reached across the table to give him a kiss on the lips.

Jack was surprised. "I didn't expect that," he laughed.

"I didn't expect you to be on my side," she admitted.

"Meghan! I'm your husband. That's what I'm here for," he swore to her. "Always. For better or for worse."

She blinked. "I know guys and their moms have some sort of special bond..."

Jack looked into her dark eyes. "Our bond is the *most* important of my life," he told her. "I love my mother, but she has been out of line. I feel like a bad husband for not stepping up and setting boundaries with her. I will do better. I love you, Meghan. You are my world, and I hate seeing you so upset."

Meghan grinned. "I love you too, Jack."

Their waitress returned with their lunches, and they dove in, oohing and aahing over the rich burgers and creamy cashew cheese. "Your mother wouldn't believe her little Jacky boy is eating vegan cheese," Meghan laughed.

"Let's leave her out of the rest of this afternoon," he begged. "This is just about *us*."

They enjoyed their meal, and as they ate, Meghan spotted Bonnie Diggs out the window. She was chatting with a man she didn't recognize, looking very friendly as they went back and forth.

"Hey, do you see that?" she asked Jack.

"Mrs. Diggs? What about her?" Jack replied.

Meghan bit her lip. "How's the investigation going?" she changed the subject. "Anything new?"

Jack raised an eyebrow. "I can't say much, as you know," he told her. "But if I could... I would tell you it's a dicey case; Mayor Rose and the police department have a really close relationship. There's talk that they are going to bring in an outside police agency to prevent any accusations of fraud."

Her dark eyes widened. "Really? So they have an eye on the Mayor?"

Jack put a finger to his lips. "I can't say."

Meghan turned to look at Bonnie, who was now walking away, arm-in-arm with the man. "What about Bonnie, babe?" she asked her husband. "Has anyone checked out Bonnie?"

She saw a shadow pass across Jack's face. He said nothing, but his expression told her what she needed to know. The police thought Bonnie Diggs had something to do with Anthony's murder. Meghan wondered if there was more to Mrs. Anthony Diggs than she had even begun to imagine.

11

The next morning, Meghan walked to work with an extra spring in her step. Snow was quietly falling as she made her way to the bakery, and delighted by its beauty, she spun herself in a silly circle, sticking out her tongue to catch a flake.

She walked into the bakery with a smile on her face, closing her eyes as she inhaled the smell of freshly baked sweet rolls.

"You look like you're off to a good start today," Trudy commented as she registered Meghan's joyful expression. "That lunch with your husband yesterday must have helped things!"

"I think it definitely helped," Pamela giggled. "Meghan didn't even come back yesterday for the end of the shift."

Meghan gave Pamela a look, but she turned to hang up her coat, the happiness returning to her face as she started humming her favorite song.

"What's gotten into you today?" Trudy inquired. "It's like you've had a few drinks or something. Oh, no... please tell me your mother-in-law hasn't driven you to drinking at nine in the morning. Meghan, do I need to be worried?"

Meghan waved her off. "It's fine," she promised Trudy, walking back to the kitchen to retrieve her yellow apron. "Sarah is home sleeping."

Trudy cocked her head to the side. "So?"

"So," Meghan continued. "She usually gets up at five in the morning to cook or do chores. This morning, for whatever reason, she slept in. I got to lay in bed with the dogs and relax for two whole hours *without* her stomping in or dropping a passive-aggressive comment... I feel like a new woman!"

Trudy nodded. "When you're young and in love, no one ever tells you that the hardest part of your marriage will be your mother-in-law..."

Meghan shrugged. "I'm not going to think about her today," she declared grandly, sweeping her arms open. "I am rested, I am in a good mood, and I am ready to bake!"

An hour later, Meghan found herself carefully stirring a bowl of blood red cake batter. She had added more coconut flour to make it thicker, and the sight of it was rather gruesome. She had a fleeting thought about Anthony Diggs, imagining his blood spilling out as he was murdered, and she choked up.

Trudy bustled into the kitchen with five dirty plates in her hands. "What is *that?*" she shrieked as she surveyed the cake batter. "It looks like you're mixing a bucket of blood!"

Meghan shook her head. "That's kind of what I was thinking," she commented. "But it isn't blood, Trudy. It's red velvet cake batter. I have a cake in the oven already, and one cooling in the refrigerator, and I added more flour to this one to make it thicker."

Trudy closed her eyes and took a deep breath. "It smells incredible," she complimented her. "I think the smell alone could take my breath away. I can't wait to see it when it's all finished."

Meghan abandoned the mixing bowl and washed her hands. "Let me get you a piece from the one that's cooling," she smiled. "Try it out for yourself."

She went into the refrigerator and retrieved the red velvet cake. She had iced it with a thick golden frosting with little flower details along the base, and she was proud of how beautiful it looked. She returned to the kitchen and cut a small piece for Trudy. "Try it."

Trudy took a small bite, and her face broke into a grin. "This is one of the best things I've ever had," she told her, licking the golden frosting from her lips. "I think if Erin and her fiance start their marriage off with something like this, they'll certainly be in for a sweet life."

Meghan thanked Trudy and put the rest of the cake back in the refrigerator. Needing to stretch her legs after sitting over the mixing bowl for so long, she went into the dining room to check on things. As she picked up a rag to wipe off some dirty tables, a rugged but good-looking man walked into the dining room. He had spiky brown hair and a lanky frame, and while he looked a bit older than Meghan, he was brimming with energy.

"That smell," he sighed as he approached the counter. "That smell is heavenly."

Meghan put the rag down and went around to the back of the counter. "How may I help you today?"

"I want whatever that smell is," he told her.

She smiled. "It isn't for sale yet," she apologized. "If you come back later, you can get some, though; it's a red velvet cake. We modified the recipes, and I think it will be incredible."

Trudy bustled through the kitchen doors holding a plated

slice of the cake. "Meghan, I cut this up for him," she told her. "Here, sir. Try some."

She handed him the plate, and he took a bite. "This is *heaven*," he moaned, his dark blue eyes closing. "You should be careful, Ma'am. Someone could be forced to commit murder for something this delicious."

Meghan laughed. "My husband is a detective in town, so I think we would be okay," she joked. "What can I do for you today?"

"I need to place a pretty big order," he explained as he bent down to study the contents of the glass counter containing the freshly baked treats. "I need fifty scones, eighteen fruit tarts, a chocolate chip muffin, ten cinnamon rolls, fifty-six danishes, and a few bagels."

She stared at him. "That's a pretty big order," she said as she rang it all up. "It will take a few minutes to prepare…"

He shook his head. "I don't need it right now," he explained. "Can you deliver it to Big Catch? The fishing tour company? The team is supposed to have an afternoon snack, and this seemed like an easy way to do it."

"I've delivered there before," she assured him. "No problem. Anthony Diggs owns—owned Big Catch. He used to have me send over desserts on Friday mornings in the winter as a special treat."

The man nodded. "I know," he told her. "I'm James Kittle, Anthony's business partner. We co-owned Big Catch, along with several of the other outdoor touring companies in the area."

"Nice to meet you," she smiled. "I'm sorry for your loss, Mr. Kittle."

"Call me James," he insisted. "And don't be sorry. Anthony was only a business partner. We weren't friends. Losing him doesn't mean a lot to me."

She blinked at him in confusion. It seemed like a strange way to accept her condolences, but as she was weighing his words, he gave her a wave. "Thanks for your help. Have a nice day."

As he exited the bakery, Trudy dashed over to her. "Did you hear that?" she whispered. "That's James Kittle."

"Anthony's business partner," Meghan chimed in, furrowing her brows. "How do you know him?"

Trudy smiled. "Everyone knows everyone around here, Meghan. You should know that by now."

Meghan watched out the window as James crossed the street and got into a shiny black Tesla. "Hmmm," she muttered.

An hour later, Erin Rogers arrived at Truly Sweet. Her ringlets were pulled up into a high bun, with two curls hanging loose, framing her face. She was dressed in a pair of skinny jeans, black knee-high boots, and a red turtleneck.

"I'm so excited for today," she announced as Trudy led her to a table set for one. "I can't wait to see what you have lined up for me."

"Prepare to be amazed," Trudy promised her. "Meghan created a lovely menu of items for you to sample."

"And if it isn't to your liking, we will make adjustments," Meghan assured her.

"Where should I begin?"

Pamela pushed a cart over to them. It was filled with small plates of desserts, and Erin's eyes widened. "This is all for me?"

"All for you," Meghan confirmed as she removed a plate of vanilla bean cake from the cart and set it in front of Erin. "Let's start with this one. It's a smooth taste, a nice way to begin."

Erin placed her napkin in her lap, smoothing it over her pants. She blinked, gently picked up the fork from the table, and guided it into the vanilla bean cake.

"Yum," she moaned as she took the first bite. "This is amazing, ladies. This vanilla flavor is so strong."

Pamela grinned. "I played around with the levels of vanilla, so I'm glad you like it."

"I really do," Erin told them as she delicately wiped her mouth with the napkin.

Meghan handed her a plate of mini eclairs. "Try this next," she urged Erin. "We thought mini eclairs would be a fun evening snack for guests to enjoy during the dancing."

Erin picked one up and took a bite, closing her eyes and savoring the taste of the thick cream filling. "It's to die for," she declared. "I think if I eat too many of these, I won't fit into my swimsuit for the honeymoon, but I don't even care. They are so good."

Trudy clapped her hands. "This is going so well," she whispered to Meghan.

"It really is," Meghan agreed as she cleared the empty plate from Erin's place and replaced it with a plate of tiramisu. "This is one of my favorite desserts to make," she told Erin. "We've worked on the ratio of coffee, rum, and ladyfingers, and I think we have perfected it."

Erin began eating the tiramisu, and her eyes widened. "This is it," she moaned. "This is what I want for my dessert. My sweetheart can have his red velvet cake, but I want this tiramisu."

"Not a problem," Meghan grinned. "We can make it happen."

They finished the tasting. Erin chose a diverse range of desserts and treats for the reception, morning after brunch, and rehearsal dinner, and Meghan was pleased by her selection.

"This has been one of the best tastings I've ever done," Erin gushed as she handed Meghan the contract she had signed. "Truly, Meghan, your work is unmatched."

Meghan beamed. "I'm so glad you think so."

"I will surely be recommending you to all my friends," Erin promised. "Gosh, you are such a gem. You should really go bigger on your advertising, Meghan. You could make a killing if you did more social media and radio marketing."

"Radio marketing?" Meghan laughed. "Do people still listen to the radio these days?"

Erin nodded earnestly. "Oh, certainly," she told her. "We use radio ads all the time for my fiance's businesses, and customers always tell us the ads are what brought them to us."

Meghan bit her lip. "Do you really think it would work?"

Erin smiled. "I think it's always worth a try!"

The front door opened, and Mrs. Sheridan, an elderly resident of Sandy Bay, bustled in. Mrs. Sheridan was known for her bold, no-nonsense attitude, and while Meghan had been intimidated by her at first, they had eventually become fond of each other.

Mrs. Sheridan hobbled over to them, balancing carefully on her cane. She had a portable radio in her other hand, and the volume was turned up obnoxiously loud.

"Mrs. Sheridan, we are in the middle of a private tasting," Trudy told her as the lyrics of a rap song filled the dining room.

Mrs. Sheridan fiddled with the buttons, and the volume increased. "What? I can't hear you," she squawked. Erin covered her ears, and Pamela shot Mrs. Sheridan a look.

"Turn it down," she told the old woman loudly, but Meghan brushed her off.

"No," she murmured. "That's it, Erin, you're right!"

"What?" Erin asked loudly.

"The radio," Meghan said to herself. "We're going on the radio!"

A fter Erin had left her tasting, Meghan fetched her coat from the back and set off toward the local radio station. She was going to drop by and see how much it would cost to do some advertising, and she was excited to see what was in store for her bakery with some new marketing.

As she made her way through the snowy streets of Sandy Bay, she thought of the press coverage the bakery had received in the past; any time she had gotten a glowing review or nice article written about her or her work, business had increased significantly for at least a month after. She wondered how business would increase after some radio advertising, and she was giddy as she imagined old and new customers flooding the dining room.

She wondered if she should mention the bakery's leap to the wedding industry; did she have enough hands on deck to handle a mass influx of wedding orders? Meghan pondered hiring a new part-time worker; she had been toying with the idea for a few months, and maybe now it was time to take action.

Meghan rounded the corner and ran right into Mayor Rose. He was walking with his wife, a petite, curvy woman with strawberry blonde hair tied in a long French braid, and the couple nearly fell as Meghan crashed into them.

"Excuse me," she apologized as she held up her hands. "I did not see you there. Forgive me for running into you."

Mrs. Rose smiled warmly at Meghan. "It's no worry at all, dear. You should be careful though; these streets were not made for running around in the winter! You're lucky we didn't go flying; last week, Mrs. Sheridan took quite a tumble after slipping on some ice, and I think she almost just met her fate."

Meghan nodded. "You're right, I was in too much of a hurry," she agreed. "I'll let you two get on your way. Nice to see you both."

Mayor Rose held up his hand. "Wait," he gestured. "Stop."

"Let her go, dear," his wife told him. "This young woman clearly has somewhere to be. She doesn't need two old folks like us taking her time."

Mayor Rose shook his head. "I just need a moment with Mrs. Irvin," he assured his wife. "Meghan, have you and your husband made up your mind? Will you be doing me the honor of voting for me in the election?"

Meghan's face paled. "The election?" she asked, her voice shaking. "Mayor Rose, your opponent just *died*. I don't think anyone is really thinking about the election right now…"

Mrs. Rose gave her husband a swat on the behind. "Roland," she chastised him. "Are you seriously asking her that? After Diggs just passed away? My goodness, dear, please forgive my rude husband. He is so… shaken… by Diggs' death. He doesn't know what he's saying."

The mayor shrugged his wife off. "I do know what I am saying," he insisted. "Look, Meghan, there is only one candidate left, and it's me. I really hoped you wouldn't make this difficult, and I don't want to cause trouble with your husband, but I think it's in your best interest to give me your endorsement."

Meghan peered at him. "And why is that?"

He stared into her dark eyes. "I could make things very difficult for the police department," he whispered to her. "And for your business, Meghan. Do you see what I am saying?"

She said nothing, and his wife interjected. "Roland Rose," Mrs. Rose screeched. "What on Earth has gotten into you? Apologize to the young woman for your rudeness. I cannot believe you. Dear, please forgive my husband. He hasn't gotten a lot of sleep lately, and he's been under a lot of stress. He has not been acting like himself, and I am so embarrassed for this outburst, I assure you."

He was silent, and Meghan nodded at Mrs. Rose. "I'll be on my way, then. My apologies again for running into you two. Have a nice day, Mayor Rose and Mrs. Rose."

Mayor Rose shouted after Meghan. "You will vote for me," he told her as she hurried away. "Like it or not, I'm the only choice for this town, Meghan!"

She took off in a sprint down the street, only slowing down when the Roses were out of sight. What had prompted the mayor's bizarre outburst? She was puzzled by his behavior, and even more worried about his threats. Why was he so concerned about the election? As she had mentioned, his only opponent was *dead*. Surely there was not a lot Mayor Rose had to worry about in his re-election campaign. Or was there?

She arrived at the radio station out of breath, still panting when she walked in and approached the receptionist's desk.

"May I help you?" the receptionist, a college aged man with a mohawk asked her.

"Who do I need to speak with about advertising?" she asked.

The man smiled. "Marty Workman, the owner," he informed her. "You're lucky; he usually isn't in at this time, but he just finished an early meeting. Shall I tell him you're here…?"

"Meghan," she told him. "Meghan Irvin. Yes, please."

Fifteen minutes later, Meghan was seated in Marty Workman's office. Marty was a tall middle-aged man with a head full of silver hair, a sleek, fitted suit, and designer shoes. Meghan instantly recognized his smooth, deep voice; he was the DJ during the late night hours on the weekends, and she had spent many long nights at the bakery listening to him.

"What can I do for you today, Meghan?" he asked with a smile. "You own that bakery, right? I've eaten a lot of your cookies over the years. My wife wants to *kill* you; she says your chocolate raspberry croissants are so good that she's put on ten pounds since you've moved to town."

Meghan grinned. "I'm glad," she told him. "Well, not that your wife wants to kill me, but I am happy she enjoys the croissants. Tell her to buy them and reheat them and add a dollop of butter on top; that's the best way to enjoy them, in my opinion."

Marty nodded. "I will give the missus that message," he promised. "So, Meghan, what brings you in today?"

"I want to do some radio advertisements for my bakery," she declared. "I want to expand our advertising, and I think this will be a great way to do it."

Marty smiled. "That will drive your business up."

"That's what I'm hoping for," she explained. "I want to do a weekly radio advertisement, if I can afford it. What does your pricing look like, Mr. Workman?"

"Please," he cracked his knuckles casually. "Call me Marty.

And pricing for a new customer as pretty as you? I think we can cut you a great deal."

Meghan shifted in her chair. Marty's compliment had made her a bit uncomfortable, but she wanted to seal the deal. "Tell me what I need to do."

"For starters, I will give you ten minutes of on air advertisement time a week," he began. "That's a lot of time. I'll also throw in a feature article in the newspaper, which I own, as well as a billboard out by the interstate."

Meghan's dark eyes grew large. "That's so much," she commented. "I don't know if I can afford all of it."

Marty reached into his desk and pulled out a pad of paper and a pen. He wrote a sum on it, folded it up, and handed it to Meghan. When she unfolded the paper, she gasped.

"This isn't enough," she protested. "You can't give me that much for so little."

He smiled wolfishly and ran a hand through his thick silver hair. "I can do whatever I want," he assured her. "I'm the owner."

Meghan stared at the slip of paper. "Why are you being so generous?" she asked in confusion. "We've just met…"

He shrugged. "I need the business," he admitted, sticking his hands in his pockets. "Maybe if a sweet little local business woman like you does some ads with me, others will follow suit. I had a bad hit this month, and things have been on a downward spiral. I need to be on the up and up, you know?"

Meghan nodded. "I get that," she told him. "If you don't mind me asking, what caused the downward spiral? Anything in particular?"

His eyes narrowed, and his face grew dark. "My business is on the brink of ruin," he sputtered angrily. "Because of him."

"Him?"

"He wouldn't pay up. He walked in here and made a lot of promises, but after months and months, he never came through on payments. He left me high and dry, Meghan. I had to take out a loan from my *grandmother* to cover expenses. Can you imagine how humiliating that was for me? He really did me dirty. And I don't like it when people do me dirty."

"Neither do I," she agreed, raising an eyebrow. "So, who was it? Who was the jerk?"

He looked right into her eyes. "Who do you think it was, Meghan?"

She felt her stomach drop, and she watched as he buried his face in his hands.

"Who hurt your business?" Meghan repeated as Marty sat back up and cleared his throat. "Who was it, Marty? What's going on here?"

"You won't believe me if I tell you."

"I will," she pleaded. "I'm a good listener, Marty. Tell me what's going on."

Marty frowned, his thick eyebrows knitting together until a deep line ran between his eyes. "It was Anthony Diggs."

She shuddered. Why was *everything* coming back to Anthony Diggs?

"What did he do?" she asked quietly. "What did Anthony Diggs do to you?"

"What *didn't* he do?" he scoffed. "I went out of my way to help him, and he really did a number on me. Diggs came to me about a year ago when he was in the early stages of planning his campaign; he was on the hunt for donors, cash, and equipment, and I said I could help him out."

Meghan pursed her lips. "Did you know him well? What about his wife?"

"Well enough," Marty commented. "He's well known in town, of course, and I've done a few trips abroad with his outdoor adventure company. They did an overseas trip a few years ago to Costa Rica, and we got to know each other down in Dominical."

"Dominical?"

"It's a sleepy little surfer village off the west coast of Costa Rica. It's hard to get to, but the food is good, the waves are insane, and the hiking is out of this world. Anthony and James led a trip down there, and I tagged along. James and I didn't see eye to eye, but Anthony and I got along well. We ended up getting beers every night of the trip. On the last day, we took off on an all-day surfing excursion down the coast. It was a blast."

Meghan nodded. "So, you guys became friends, and then he came to you and asked for help with his campaign?"

"He wanted equipment, airtime, billboards, and the works," Marty explained as he stood up and began to pace around his office. "He wanted it all. And I was the trusting dummy who practically threw my time and money at him. I should have known better. Anyone who makes promises to a *friend* and doesn't deliver on those promises is the scum of the earth."

She cocked her head to the side. "So then what happened?"

"He really got me good, Meghan; he had all of these dreams and plans about the campaign, but when it was time to pay up, he always bailed."

"Why didn't you stop providing stuff for him? Didn't you realize he was swindling you? You seem pretty savvy to me, Marty…"

Marty glowered at her. "It's not that simple," he promised. "He had me running all sorts of orders and errands, and he kept promising me the money was coming. Or, he would write a small check to hold me over, promising there would be more money when he was elected."

She frowned. "There never was any money, was there?"

Marty crossed his arms and perched on the edge of his desk. "He was a con artist," he spat as Meghan's dark eyes grew large. "He really got me. He sold me this vision of how the media could have a positive impact on the prosperity of Sandy Bay. I'm a good guy, Meghan. I like to help people, and I love this town. I was inspired to make large orders for his business and his campaign. But now, in the end…"

She stared at him. "What about suing his estate?" she asked quietly. "I know that's a big step, but you can't let your business go under for his mistakes."

Marty sighed. "I already contacted his attorney," he informed her, his voice flat. "There's no money left. He went through it all. Apparently, Anthony had a little gambling problem, and all of the Diggs' money is gone."

She stared at him. "Do you think Bonnie knew?" she whispered, thinking of the elegantly dressed widow in her designer clothes.

"She knows now," Marty laughed. "Her husband was a *loser* and a cheat, and I'm sure if he's done me wrong, he's done *her* wrong. It sounds like that piece of trash deserved what happened to him, if you ask me. Then again, Bonnie is just as bad as he was, if not worse."

She raised both eyebrows. "What do you mean, Marty? What did Bonnie do?"

He shook his head. "She is conniving," he warned her. "She comes off as sweet and quaint with that pretty face and those nice clothes, but beneath it all, she is a *killer*. When Anthony died, she lawyered up faster than you can imagine, Meghan. What does that tell you? And I'm not talking about a silly little Sandy Bay attorney. I'm talking about the big dogs. She hired one of the best attorneys in Los Angeles to fly up here and sort through her husband's mess. Don't you think that screams guilty?"

Meghan was shocked by the hostility in his tone. "I'm sorry all of this happened to you," she offered quietly. "I can see you are really upset. I'll just get out of your hair, now."

He walked her to the door. "Are we in for our deal?" he asked, and she could smell a faint sour scent on his breath. Had he been drinking in the middle of the day? She knew he was having problems, but was there more to Marty than she knew?

"I think so," she told him. "I'll talk to my husband about it, as well as my team at the bakery. If all goes well, I will have the money wired to you tomorrow."

Marty stared at her. "Tonight, would be better," he insisted. "Can you wire the money tonight?"

She felt her stomach churn. Marty had been charming at first, but now, he was making her feel apprehensive. "I'll do my best," she told him, and she turned and left the radio station as fast as she could.

As she walked outside, she could not get over her conversation with Marty; Anthony had always presented himself as a respectable gentleman, so professional and refined. Could he really be as malicious as Marty had described?

Her phone buzzed, and she reached into her pocket to retrieve it, smiling as she realized the text message was from her husband.

Date night tonight?

She texted back immediately.

YES!!

Her heart was glowing as she imagined a romantic date

with Jack; she started thinking of all the outfits in her closet, determining which would look best on her for their date. Should she wear the plum midi skirt and matching top, or the blush turtleneck dress with her camel boots?

I want to do something exciting. You've been talking about trying new things and new experiences....Want to try something new?

She thought for a moment. What had she and Jack not done before in Sandy Bay? They had gone bowling, to the movies, walked dogs at the shelter, taken a dance class, and tried every restaurant in town. She wondered if Jack had something special up his sleeve.

Her phone buzzed again.

I don't have anything in mind, but if you think of something, let me know.

Meghan continued her walk, catching sight of a new billboard that had been put up a few yards away. "That's new," she thought to herself as she squinted her eyes to see what was on it. "Big Catch Outdoor Tours."

The sign featured a laughing couple dressed in matching fishing attire. "They look like they're having fun," she observed. "Maybe this is the perfect coincidence. Jack and I have never done an outdoor adventure tour. I wonder if he would be into that?"

She imagined herself and Jack dressed in matching fishing attire, both happily riding the waves aboard a fishing boat. Would she enjoy deep-sea fishing? She had only done it a few times, but she knew Jack loved outdoor activities, and he loved being on the water more than anything in the world.

Before she could ask him if he would like to do an excursion, she heard a scream from inside Big Catch Outdoor Tours, followed by loud, guttural sobs. Meghan didn't think twice; she darted into the office, following the sound of the wailing. She didn't know what was going on, but she was going to find out.

M eghan stormed into the building. It was rustic, with large timber beams running up and down the length of the ceiling, and black leather furniture tucked into the corners. A massive reclaimed wooden desk sat in the center of the room, and a burly male receptionist sat behind it.

"Can I help you?" he asked as she approached him.

"What's going on in here?" she demanded. "Where is that screaming and crying coming from?"

He peered at her in curiosity. "Ma'am, we're closed right now," he informed her. "You can take a business card if you'd like, but we are closed for business until two."

She turned as she heard the crying continue, and she scurried past the receptionist who was trying to wave her down.

"Ma'am," he called after her as she marched down a hallway toward the loud crying. "Do you have an appointment? We require appointments to meet with staff! We don't open until two!"

Meghan burst into a room at the end of the hallway.

James Kittle, along with five uniformed staff members, were staring at her. They were seated around a large wooden conference table with several boxes of *her* desserts in front of them. She saw their faces were drawn, and they looked confused as she stood in the middle of the room.

"Meghan?" James asked, standing up and coming over to greet her. He was wearing khaki pants, a white Henley shirt, and a red vest, and he looked every bit the picture of the owner of an outdoor adventure company. "Nice to see you. Were we expecting you today?"

She stared at the group of employees. "What's going on here?" she demanded, balling her hands into fists. "I was walking outside when I heard screaming coming from this building."

James wiped his eyes. "We were just taking a lunch break," he sighed as he waved off the staff members. "Go get back to work, guys. I'll see you in a few minutes."

"Why are people screaming over lunch?" she wondered as the group dispersed.

He hung his head. "A few of the staffers wanted to share stories about Anthony during our lunch hour" he explained quietly. "It's been really hard on some of them, and with Bonnie putting off the funeral, they haven't had a chance to grieve. Anthony meant a lot to some of these guys; he was like a big brother to them, and they need to have the time and space to mourn him."

Meghan stared at him. "Wait... Bonnie put off the funeral? What do you mean? Isn't his funeral scheduled for next week at the Episcopalian church? There was an announcement in the paper this morning about it."

James scowled. "I don't want to start rumors or speak ill of the newly widowed Mrs. Diggs, but she's being really strange about all of it," he told her. "Look, I'll be honest with you, Meghan. Anthony wasn't always the standup guy he pretended to be, and Bonnie had to deal with a lot during their marriage. I don't blame her for being angry and canceling his funeral; I can only imagine if I had a husband who was that shady, I would be happy as a clam if he dropped dead..."

"Like what? What kind of shady things did he do, James?"

He frowned. "He was my friend and business partner, but I knew the real Anthony better than anyone. Infidelity. Fraud. Addiction. He certainly had his vices, to say the least. Shall I go on?"

Her eyes grew large, and she shook her head.

"I thought that would be enough," he commented, sitting back down in his chair at the head of the table. "Anyway, when Anthony died, a lot of angry people came out of the woodwork. They're going after his money, and all sorts of secrets about him are coming out. Bonnie is understandably upset, and from what I've heard, she's canceled his funeral."

Meghan bit her lip. "She's that angry with him? Bonnie is angry enough to *cancel* his funeral?"

James shrugged. "It's some pretty dark stuff, Meghan," he told her. "Can you imagine if you found out this kind of messy information about your husband after he died? I'm sure you wouldn't be inclined to throw a big, fancy funeral for him, would you?"

She shook her head. "No, I guess I wouldn't."

He put a friendly hand on her arm. "If you're wondering, Anthony and I were total opposites," he declared. "I am loyal and honest, and I love my girl more than anything."

"How did you and Anthony get hooked up for your business?" she asked. "If you two are so different, how could you be friends?"

He smiled. "You're asking how I could be friends with someone so... troubled? Shady? Ruthless?"

"Yes."

He sighed. "Anthony and I go way back," he told her. "Our mothers were friends; they were both Italian gals who moved to America around the same time. They both married handsome GIs—our dads—and moved to Sandy Bay after the war. They didn't speak much English, and they hit it off when they both realized they weren't the only Italian woman in the neighborhood."

"I love Italy," Meghan commented. "I spent a summer studying in Sarzana and fell in love with the food."

He grinned. "My mother's ribollita was to die for," he promised her. "Authentic Italian food is a gift from the Heavens. Anyway, our mothers were close, so we grew up together. We were like brothers when we were little boys, these two Italian American boys in Sandy Bay, just trying to figure out who we were and what we wanted to do with our lives.

She nodded. "Childhood friends..."

"Exactly," he affirmed. "But we grew up, and I stayed around town for college while Anthony went to Yale. He thought he was a big deal for making it into an Ivy League school. He ended up coming back right after graduation when his Ma died. It broke his heart, Meghan. He was a broken man when he lost his Ma."

"I can imagine," she replied softly. "Mothers are irreplaceable."

"Yes, they are," he agreed. "Mine was a saint, God rest her soul. When my Ma died, I was upset, but I knew life went on. I knew I had to make her proud by making something of myself. That's when Anthony and I started the business. When his Ma died, poor Anthony tried to drown his sadness in booze and women, and it just never stopped."

"Even when he married Bonnie?"

"Bonnie," he rolled his eyes. "She's a crutch and an

VELVET CAKE AND MURDER

enabler. I've tried to tell Bonnie about Anthony's problems for years, and she just didn't want to hear it."

She nodded, but said nothing, watching as he ran his hand through his hair.

"Say, I have to get back to work, but is there anything else you need? I'll certainly be back at the bakery to order more treats for the staff, but in the meantime, are we good?"

"I'm fine, thanks," she told him as she backed out of the room. "Sorry to interrupt like that. I guess my nerves are a little out of whack with Anthony's murder…"

As Meghan walked home, she thought about what James had told her about Anthony, as well as her conversation with Marty. Anthony sounded like a pathological liar, someone who thought nothing of causing trouble. She felt strange thinking of all the times they had interacted; she had thought he was a clean cut, kind, decent man, but from what she had been told, she had clearly been fooled.

She wondered about Bonnie, too. Bonnie, with her blonde hair and gorgeous clothes, was an enigma. Had Bonnie known the extent of her husband's issues? Was she *part* of Anthony's schemes, complicit in his wrong-doings? She didn't know, but she had a bad feeling that the quiet, shy widow was not as innocent as she thought.

When she made it back to the bakery, she shivered, feeling the freezing winter air bite into her skin through her coat. The sun was quickly setting, and thick, heavy darkness was quickly covering the neighborhood. Meghan could hear the crash of the nearby ocean, and she shuddered as she imagined herself and Jack on a fishing boat. Perhaps winter was not the best time for an outdoor excursion after all.

As she neared the front door, she heard shouting from around the corner. A crowd was gathered outside of the bakery, and she hurried over to see what the commotion was all about.

"What's going on?" she asked as she shoved through the crowd. "Excuse me? Excuse me?"

She noticed there were several police cars parked nearby, and she spotted uniformed officers patrolling the group. "What is happening?" she thought as she moved past a woman carrying a baby on her hip.

"The mayor is being arrested," an older woman told Meghan as Mayor Rose was led out of the bakery in hand-cuffs, his wife running behind them, weeping.

"For what?" Meghan asked in shock, looking through the crowd to see if she recognized any of the police officers. "What did he do?"

"No one will give us a clear answer," a man told her as he jostled by.

The Mayor's face was red with anger, and Meghan's heart sank as she registered the heartbroken expression on his wife's face. She stared at them, watching as the two officers led him to a police car.

"This isn't the end for me," he shouted as he was carefully helped into the vehicle. "This isn't the end. I am still your mayor, citizens of Sandy Bay! I am still fighting for you. You can't get rid of me just yet, mark my words!"

15

M eghan tore away from the crowd and ran into the bakery. There were no customers in the dining room, but her two employees were both there.

"What is going on out there?" she gasped, finding Trudy and Pamela both pressed against the windows, staring as the police cars drove away.

Trudy's face was drawn. "The mayor was just arrested," she told her, a worried look in her eyes. "They took Mayor Rose away, Meghan."

"Well, I know that," Meghan exclaimed, slightly out of breath from all the excitement. "But what *happened* in the bakery? I was told he was arrested *here!*"

Pamela took a deep breath. "It was crazy," she told Meghan. "I was cleaning the windows out here," she began, nervously playing with the ends of her hair as she shifted back and forth. "I was just about to start drying the big window facing main street when I saw police lights outside."

"Police lights? Outside of the bakery?"

She nodded. "They pulled the Mayor over. I figured it was

to tell him government business or to get his signature or something. I didn't think he was in trouble. Anyway, I went outside to see if they wanted to try some of our red velvet cupcakes; I accidentally made too many this morning, and I wanted to give the extras to the police officers."

Meghan raised an eyebrow. "So then what happened next?"

Pamela's face fell. "It got ugly," she whispered. "It was so scary, Meghan. I thought he was going to hurt me. The look in his eyes was terrifying, and if the police hadn't been there..."

Trudy pursed her lips. "Pamela put a bunch of the cupcakes into a basket to take out to them. It really was a nice idea, Meghan. She can be so thoughtful sometimes."

"So, what went wrong?" she asked. "With the Mayor? Why was Pamela so scared?"

Pamela scowled. "The Mayor started yelling at me, Meghan. He positioned himself so that he was standing right over me. It was awful. He said the bakery was a failure, and that you are a shady character. That made me so angry, Meghan; he can't talk about you like that! I started talking back to him, and he got up in my face."

Meghan's eyes widened. "The Mayor got in your face? Oh, Pamela. I am so sorry."

She shrugged. "The police stepped in right away," she told her. "They told him to back off and leave me alone, but he just kept going. He wouldn't stop; it was like he was out of his mind or something. They finally had to take him down. I got out of the way, and they wrestled him to the ground and put handcuffs on him."

Trudy crossed her arms over her chest. "Roland Rose is off his rocker," she declared. "Who does that, yelling at a young woman on the street like that? It was disgusting. His wife was right there, too. She looked mortified, but she didn't step in. She easily could have stopped it. I saw the whole thing, and so did everyone else who was nearby. The Mayor's reputation is ruined, that's for sure."

Meghan turned back to Pamela. "Are you okay? Did he hurt you? Do we need to call a doctor, or your parents?"

"I feel shaken," Pamela said. "But please don't call a doctor, or my parents. I'm fine. I don't want anyone to worry about me. It was wild that they arrested him; a crowd gathered, and they took him away."

Just then, the front doors opened, and Mrs. Rose walked in. Her strawberry blonde hair was piled atop her head in a tight bun, and her hands were clenched into fists.

"Mrs. Rose," Meghan said softly. "Can we help you? We are so sorry about what happened."

Mrs. Rose narrowed her eyes at her. "You're *sorry?*" she said mockingly. "Sorry? It's your fault that we are in this situation."

Meghan stared at her. "My fault? What? What do you mean?"

Mrs. Rose pointed at her, her index finger only an inch away from Meghan's nose. "My husband has done so much for you," she began, her voice shaking. "He supported your bakery, he spoke highly of you, and he helped bring business to you. He did a lot for you, and what did you do? You didn't promise him your vote!"

Meghan's dark eyes widened. "Mrs. Rose," she said softly. "I appreciate everything your husband has done for me and for my business. I truly do. But democracy isn't about favors and owing others. It is about making your own decisions and choosing candidates who best represent you and your interests. I honestly had not decided on who I was voting on, but I am sorry that has caused distress with your husband."

Mrs. Rose frowned at her. "The lack of support from people like you, people my husband has helped and supported, has *broken* him; he has been devastated by the lack of support from all the people and businesses he has worked with in the past, and this has sent him over the edge. You have *ruined* my husband, Mrs. Irvin. Shame on you."

Trudy stepped in. "Back off," she ordered, forcing Mrs. Rose to take a few steps back. "You need to leave this bakery immediately. You aren't going to talk to Meghan like that. She hasn't done anything to deserve it."

Mrs. Rose laughed. "She's ruined my life," she insisted, walking away from Trudy and following Meghan across the dining room. "She ruined my husband, and she's ruined my life."

Trudy furrowed her brow. "You need to go," she said firmly, reaching for Mrs. Rose's elbow. "You need to leave immediately. This is inappropriate and unfair."

Mrs. Rose stomped her foot. "I have every right to be here," she declared. "You can't force me to leave. I'm the mayor's wife. You can't make me do *anything.*"

"But I can."

Their heads turned, and Meghan breathed a sigh of relief as Jack walked into the bakery. He was dressed in his uniform, and his face was dark as he walked up to the women. "What's going on here?"

Mrs. Rose forced herself to smile. "I was just getting a treat," she lied, turning to gesture at the front counter. "It's been a long day, and I need a bite to eat."

Jack turned to his wife. "Is that true?" he asked Meghan. "What is going on here?"

Pamela rushed over to Jack. "Mrs. Rose was trying to attack Meghan!" she shrieked, waving her hands frantically. "She was trying to hurt your wife, Detective Irvin."

Mrs. Rose gasped. "That simply is not true," she promised Jack, her face pinched. "I merely came in here to inquire about some treats, and these ladies started going off on me. I had nothing to do with any trouble."

Jack looked at Meghan. "Honey?"

Meghan shook her head. "She's lying," she whispered to her husband. "Please have her removed, dear."

Jack silently took Mrs. Rose arm and led her out of the bakery. "Why are you doing this?" she moaned as Jack escorted her out onto the sidewalk. "I was just visiting the bakery. There was no harm done!"

Jack came back inside with a scowl on his face. "What was that all about? Are you all okay?"

Meghan pursed her lips. "She came in here ranting and raving about her husband," she explained to Jack as Trudy and Pamela nodded. "She thinks her husband's downfall is somehow my fault, babe. She thinks I "broke" him, and that my lack of support sent Mayor Rose over the edge."

Jack studied her face. "What do you think about that?"

"I think it's insane," she told him. "Mayor Rose's issues are not my fault; I hadn't even decided who I was voting for before Anthony died. My parents taught me to never discuss politics. In the South, we consider it quite rude to talk about politics with anyone other than your spouse, so even if I had made up my mind about who I was voting for, I wasn't going to tell anyone besides you."

"That's the way to do it," Trudy chimed in. "Politics are no one else's business."

"Yeah!" Pamela added, though she was not quite old enough to vote.

Jack sighed. "Do you want to press charges against her?" he asked his wife, pulling out his notepad and pen. "I can charge her for harassment, but it is up to you. You have two witnesses, so it is a strong case, but given the town is up in arms about this murder case, I don't know how much attention a harassment charge against the mayor's wife would garner right now."

She shook her head. "Don't do it," she instructed him. "I don't want to press charges. I just want them to leave me alone. The look in Mrs. Rose eyes was creepy; it was as if she had been possessed. And the way he cornered Pamela? The Mayor seems more dangerous than I thought, Jack. I'm worried."

"Then maybe a restraining order against both of them," he suggested. "I can get that filed for you in a jiff, babe. What do you think?"

Meghan nodded. "That seems more appropriate," she agreed. "I just want this mess to be over. I don't want to have to worry about angry mayors and murderers."

"They might be one and the same," he murmured to her, pulling her close and moving her hair back to whisper into her ear.

"What do you mean?" she asked in alarm. "Jack, do you mean the mayor murdered Anthony?"

Jack's blue eyes were filled with concern. "I can't quite say," he told her softly. "But we've found some major evidence to show that the mayor was discussing a hit on Anthony."

"To kill him?" she gasped.

"Exactly," her husband affirmed. "We still have a lot of work to do on the case, but from what we gathered, it looks like Mayor Rose's arrest today was a lucky thing; I suspect he knows a lot more about Anthony Diggs' murder than he's letting on, and if I'm not mistaken, I think he did it himself."

16

T hat evening, when Meghan returned home, she was in need of a quiet night; after the incident with Mayor Rose and Mrs. Rose, she felt exhausted, drained from the stress of being yelled at and worried about how Pamela was doing. All she wanted to do was relax, take a hot bath, and drink a glass of red wine.

When she stepped through the front door, she was horrified to find her living room had been redone *again*, though this time, the changes were much more dramatic than the original makeover Sarah had done. The walls had been repainted mauve, the couch and armchair had been covered with mint green linen with a variety of brown throw pillows resting on top. There was a giant round beige and purple rug on the floor, and the coffee table had been brought back, though it was stained a deep shade of mahogany that did not match any of the finishings in the house.

She glanced around looking for her dogs, furious when she heard barking from outside. She rushed to the back door and threw it open; all three dogs hurried inside, with Fiesta and Siesta shivering from the cold.

"Sarah?" she cried out angrily as she picked up Siesta and held her to her chest. "Sarah? Are you here?"

Sarah came down the stairs wearing a pink bathrobe and slippers, her hair wrapped up in a towel. "Why are you shouting?" she asked as Meghan narrowed her eyes. "I am trying to relax in the bathtub, Meghan. Is the shouting necessary?"

Meghan placed Siesta on the floor and put her hands on her hips. "Yes," she began. "I think shouting is necessary, Sarah. What happened to the living room?"

Sarah smiled, her bright blue eyes crinkling as she clapped her hands in excitement. "Don't you love it?" she asked. "I thought the mauve looked nice with the ceilings. That other color you had was so dull, Meghan. A lady never wants her living room to be perceived as dull."

Meghan stomped her foot, surprising even herself with the outburst. "I *liked* the beige walls we had before," she insisted. "I selected the color myself, Sarah. And you changed it without asking!"

Sarah crossed her arms. "I don't like your tone," she commented as Meghan's face reddened. "It's not becoming."

"You aren't my mother," Meghan declared, throwing her arms open and gesturing at the living room. "And you aren't the lady of this house. You don't have the right to make decisions about our home, Sarah. It's my house. Mine and Jack's. And *we* decide what changes get to be made, not you."

Sarah stared at Meghan. "That tone," she clucked. "Truly, I don't know what's gotten into you. Jack told me to make myself at home, and I thought some little changes would be lovely. I thought you would be grateful for my help, and clearly that is not the case, Meghan."

Meghan clenched her hands into fists, the anger rising and swelling in her chest. "Sarah, Jack and I are a married couple," she continued. "We are married to each other. We are adults, and we are in charge of this house. Any changes need to be run by us. You can't just show up at my work, you can't just paint the walls, and you can't stick my dogs outside in the middle of a cold winter evening."

Sarah pursed her lips. "Someone is a little angry."

"A little angry? I am livid, Sarah. I have held my tongue about your comments and meddling for the last week and a half, but I can't do it anymore. You have to respect me. I don't know what I have to do to earn your respect, but I need you to tell me so we can both just get along and move on."

Jack walked into the room with a pained look on his face. "What's happening? Meghan? Why are you speaking to my mother that way?"

Sarah pouted, sticking her lips out and batting her eyelashes. "She's been cross with me during this entire visit," she complained. "And now, she's verbally abusing me, Jack. It isn't right to let your wife speak to your mother like that."

Meghan gasped. "Jack, go look at our living room!"

"I saw it," he admitted, his lips turning downward into a frown.

"And?" she asked. "And what are you going to do about it? Your mother has no boundaries, and her meddling is hurting our marriage."

Jack stared at her. "I spoke with my mom about interfering with the household decor and showing up at your work," he told her quietly. "And mom, Meghan is happy you are here. She just needs you to back off a bit with making changes."

Sarah smiled. "Of course, dear. Whatever you say."

He turned to Meghan. "See? It's all better."

Meghan shook her head. "I need her to apologize," she insisted. "I need her to recognize that she's been out of line."

"I'm not taking sides anymore," he announced, turning on

his heel and striding away. "You two need to work this out yourselves."

Meghan and Sarah stared as he walked into the living room and sat down on the couch. He turned on the television and began watching a basketball game.

Meghan tiptoed into the room and sat down next to him, and Sarah followed. They sat on both sides of him, all three Irvins sitting in silence as the announcer called out plays.

"I can make some popcorn?" Meghan quietly suggested. "For all of us? I'll even add caramel and salt—your favorite toppings, Jack."

Sarah cleared her throat. "How about I make dinner for all of us?" she suggested. "I can make steak and macaroni—your favorites, Jack. And I'll make fresh popcorn with caramel, salt, and *butter*. I know *those* are your favorite toppings, dear."

Meghan frowned. She rose from her seat. "I'll go pick up dinner for us from Urchins Paradise!" she told them. "We'll do seafood and treats."

Sarah laughed. "Jack doesn't like seafood," she said snarkily. "You should probably know that about him, Meghan."

"ENOUGH," Jack boomed. "That is enough. You are both acting like children. Mom, you have to back off of the decorating and the little comments about Meghan. She's a great wife and takes good care of me, and she is my highest priority. Meghan, you have to stop letting my mom get to you. She is who she is, and if you take it too personally, you are going to lose your mind. My mom means well, and you need to see the good in her."

He stood up and walked out of the room, leaving Meghan and Sarah to stare at each other. "I'm sorry," Sarah finally broke the silence, sitting back down and burying her head in her hands. "I don't have any daughters, Meghan, and my own mother was a monster. She constantly put me down and criticized me, and it's all I know how to do. I'm sorry. You are a lovely woman, and Jack is lucky to have you. I am lucky to have you as a daughter-in-law."

Meghan blinked. "Really?"

"Really," Sarah agreed. "I can only imagine I've been a bit of a pain for you, and you are right: I don't have a lot of boundaries, and that is a problem I need to work on. I'm sorry."

Meghan's heart warmed. Sarah was being genuine and kind, and Meghan had never heard her be this candid before.

"I'm sorry, too," she apologized quietly, reaching over to take Sarah's hand and give it a squeeze. "I could have been more patient with you, and I wasn't honest about how I felt about things you did to the house. I could have spoken up and saved us both a lot of heartache."

Sarah smiled weakly. "Can this be our truce?" she asked, her eyes filling with tears. "Can we start over? I want us to get along, and I want to be a mother-in-law you love and enjoy, not one that makes you cringe."

Meghan nodded. "I think this is our truce," she agreed. "Let's start fresh, Sarah. This is our new beginning, and you are always welcome in our home."

That night, after the three Irvins had eaten takeout pizza (Jack's idea) and watched an 80s romance (Sarah's idea), Meghan and Jack settled onto the pullout couch to go to sleep.

"That was the kind of family night I've been dreaming about," Jack grinned as he pulled Meghan into his arms. "You and my mom are like two peas in a pod. I think you two will grow into good friends."

"I think we will too," Meghan smiled back at him, feeling her spirits lift. "Do you have a busy day tomorrow?" she asked.

"I do," he told her, leaning over to give her a peck on the cheek. "The Diggs investigation is taking a lot more time than I expected, and I probably won't be home until eight or nine."

"What's going on, anyway?" she asked. "You said you had some more information about the mayor?"

"You know I can't tell you," he told her, kissing her on the nose. "But if I could, I would tell you that a man arrested in Nevada on unrelated charges gave us some useful information."

"What did he say?" she asked. "A man in Nevada?"

"The state police got him for a drug charge," he explained. "And he offered to spill some secrets about other crimes to decrease his charges. He had a lot of cash on him, too, and he said he had gotten it from Roland Rose."

"Our Mayor?" she gasped. "Seriously?"

"That's what this guy said," Jack confirmed. "The Mayor had been making some big payments to this guy. The last payment, from what we can tell, came the day before Diggs was killed."

The color drained from her face. "You're kidding."

"It was all in black and white," Jack told her. "Though we found something else…"

"What is it?"

"We found a message from the mayor to this guy," he told her quietly. "The message urged the guy not to do it. He didn't specify what the *it* was, but he said don't do it."

"That doesn't mean anything," Meghan sighed. "Especially not if you have evidence of payments between them."

Jack frowned. "There's a problem, though," he told her. "That guy in Nevada? There's a paper trail that tells us he wasn't in Sandy Bay on the night Diggs was murdered. He was in Panama City, Florida. We have video and bank statements to prove it."

"So, what you're saying is…"

"What I'm saying is that the Mayor has some shady stuff going on," Jack told her matter-of-factly. "But we aren't sure if that includes murder."

Meghan's stomach twisted into a knot. "So, if the Mayor didn't do it," she wondered aloud. "Who killed Anthony Diggs?"

17

"If we don't add the cream filling, it will be *ruined*!"

It was early the next morning, and Meghan, Trudy, and Pamela were standing over three plates of red velvet cake. Erin had emailed them some notes about the tasting, and she had requested some adjustments be made to the red velvet cake.

"I don't think it's the filling," Meghan protested, gesturing at the cake. "I don't think she liked the coconut flour. It's an easy fix, ladies; we will just use almond flour instead. Almond flour is the most similar to regular flour, and I think that will do the trick."

Trudy lifted a fork to her mouth and took a bite. "The flavor is so rich," she smiled, chewing slowly. "Adding milk to the recipe was a great idea, Pamela."

"I'm just worried about the filling," Pamela repeated. "Erin's notes said that it could use a little something. I think we should reconsider using the cream cheese filling."

Just then, a familiar voice filled the dining room. "Karen's here," Meghan murmured, putting her fork down and wiping her hands on her apron. "I'll be right back, ladies. I'm going to run out and say hello."

"Wait," Pamela called out. "Take a slice of the cake. Maybe Karen will have an idea."

Meghan smiled and took a plate of the red velvet cake. "Great idea, Pamela."

She walked into the dining room with a wide grin on her face, happy to see her good friend. Though they were decades apart in age, Karen and Meghan had become fast friends when they had met in Los Angeles a few years ago. Karen was a retired nurse living in the same building as Meghan, and they had instantly connected. When Karen had left Los Angeles and returned to her hometown of Sandy Bay, she invited Meghan to come with her. On a whim, Meghan had decided to join her friend, and thanks to Karen, she was now happily living and working in the Pacific Northwest.

"What brings you in this morning?" Meghan asked as Karen wiped her brow.

Dressed in a pair of velour jogging pants and a matching jacket, Karen smiled and flexed her biceps. "I was just finishing a jog," she told Meghan. "I was feeling a little low blood sugar, and I popped in for a treat."

"You came to the right place," Meghan told her. "I have something special for you to try."

"Is it vegan?" Karen asked in alarm as she looked at the cake.

"We added a splash of milk," Meghan admitted. "Can you deal with it, or should I grab a vegan bagel for you?"

Karen held the plate to her face and inhaled. "I think I can make this work," she smiled. "It smells amazing, Meghan."

Meghan gave her a fork, and Karen took a bite. "This is the best thing I've ever tried," she praised as Meghan beamed.

"You could convince me to end my veganism for cake like this. It's incredible."

"I'm glad you like it," Meghan told her. "We're working on the recipe and making adjustments, but I think this might be the final recipe we work with."

"It's divine," Karen praised. "I don't think it could be any better."

A woman examining desserts at the counter turned to look at them. "Is that red velvet cake?" she asked Meghan. "I would love some of that. It smells so good."

Meghan turned and called out to the kitchen. "Pamela? How many slices do we have left of the red velvet cake?"

"Two slices left," the teenager replied.

Meghan nodded at the woman. "We can have one sent to your table in a just a moment."

A man barreled over with a five-dollar bill in his hand. "Red velvet cake? I didn't know you had that in stock. I want some," he insisted, slapping the cash into Meghan's hand. "Take this. Keep the change."

Meghan smiled. "Have a seat and we'll bring it right out."

A woman with two small children came over and tugged on Meghan's sleeve. "I heard you have red velvet cake?" she asked. "My kids want some. Can I order a slice?"

Meghan bit her lip. "We just sold our last two pieces for the day," she explained apologetically. "I am so sorry. If you come back tomorrow, you can have a fresh slice."

The woman stared at her. "It's for my kids," she repeated, gesturing at the two elementary-aged children with her. "Come on, lady. Surely you have another slice? Or, I can give you ten dollars for the last slice. I saw that guy only gave you five."

She pressed a ten-dollar bill into Meghan's hand. "Come on. Take my money. My kids have been begging for cake, and you'll be doing me a favor."

"I'm sorry," Meghan told her. "I already sold our last two slices."

The woman angrily marched over to the man who was waiting for his cake. "This is your fault," she screeched. "You don't have kids with you. Give me the slice of cake. My kids want it. It's not like you need it, anyway."

He rose from his seat. "Excuse me?"

"You could stand to lose some weight," she continued. "Just let me buy that slice of cake. Come on, man."

He glowered at her. "Walk away, lady."

"Or what?"

"Hey," Meghan interjected, moving to stand between them. "Please stop this. I don't want to ask you to leave, but I am going to have to take action if you two continue this."

"She started it," the man pointed at the woman. "I was just sitting here minding my own business and she started harassing me."

The woman glared at him. "Can't you do a mother a favor? Is it that hard to be a good person these days?"

She tried to dart past Meghan to get closer to the man, but Meghan held her ground. "Ma'am, please take your kids and go home," she asked politely. "Please."

The front door opened, and James Kittle strode in. "I heard the shouting from the street," he announced as he put a hand on the woman's arm. "What's going on? If Mrs. Irvin asked you to leave, you need to go."

The woman pursed her lips, but she gathered her children and left the bakery.

"Thank you," Meghan told him, thankful for the help. "She was quite riled up…"

"Tensions are high in town," he shrugged. "Don't take it too personally. Anyway, I wanted to drop by and get things settled for the fishing trip," he told her. "Your husband sent over a payment, and he wanted me to check with you about dates and times. Can we talk?"

Her eyes lit up. "My husband?"

"He arranged an excursion for you two," he explained. "As a date night."

She remembered Jack's text message from a few days ago and grinned. "That was thoughtful of him," she remarked, imagining her husband sorting out the details with James. "What do you need from me, exactly?"

"Your preferred dates and times," he told her with a smile. "He said you're a busy person, and he wanted you to pick a day and time that worked best for your schedule."

Meghan nodded. "I don't have time to go through my calendar right now," she apologized. "Can I reach out to you later today with that information?"

"No worries!" he assured her as he waved goodbye. "Call me anytime."

On her lunch break, she felt her back tighten, and she grimaced as she thought of all the time she had spent that day sitting. Meghan liked to move her body and stay active, and she had been huddled over a mixing bowl for the better part of her day.

"I'll check my schedule and walk over to Big Catch," she decided as she looked through the calendar on her cell phone and selected a few dates and times that would work for the excursion with Jack. "If I walk there and back, I can get some fresh air and help these stiff legs."

As she set off toward Big Catch, she felt joyful as she thought about the date Jack had planned. Things were going much better with Sarah, Jack had been in a good mood, and now, she was happily enjoying time outside as she headed over to the store to plan their date. Despite the chaos in town surrounding the mayor and Anthony's murder, Meghan felt a glimmer of hope in her heart, and she happily made her way down the street.

She rounded the corner and turned onto Washington Street, one of the main streets in town. She looked down at her watch and realized the walk was taking longer than expected, and she ducked off onto New York Street for a little shortcut. The road was less populated, and she moved with ease across the freshly plowed sidewalks.

As Meghan walked down New York Street, she spotted a familiar figure ahead of her. Dressed in a pair of red wide leg silk trousers and a matching coat, her hair tied back in a low knot, was Mrs. Anthony Diggs.

"Bonnie," Meghan murmured as she moved closer to her. Bonnie was not alone; she stood with a tall man Meghan had never seen before, and as Meghan drew close enough to see him clearly, they embraced.

"Who is that?" she wondered, but before she could approach them, she was stopped.

"What kind of trouble are you causing today? Shouldn't you be at home with your husband?"

She groaned. It was Mrs. Sheridan. She smiled politely, but inwardly, she was furious. What was Bonnie up to? Who was the man she was with? Could Mrs. Sheridan have picked a worse time to interfere?

"I want to give you some feedback," Mrs. Sheridan croaked as Meghan forced herself to smile. "About your desserts."

"What's that, Mrs. Sheridan?"

Mrs. Sheridan stared at her. "I've never liked your desserts," she told her with a straight face. "They have always been too sweet or too ugly. They haven't tickled my fancy."

"I'm sorry to hear that," Meghan sighed, making every effort to be cordial.

"But then, I heard about your red velvet cake," her eyes

glittered. "I love red velvet cake. My mother used to make it for me when I was a girl. I want to place an order with you for a red velvet cake, and I want it by tomorrow morning."

Meghan laughed, but Mrs. Sheridan did not. "You're serious?"

"As a heart attack," she said solemnly. "I want a red velvet cake, and I want it badly."

Meghan exhaled. "I will let the girls at the bakery know," she promised. "I have to go, but I will see you tomorrow."

"Wait!" Mrs. Sheridan called out after her, but Meghan hurried away. Bonnie and the man were walking down the street, and Meghan had to follow them.

They turned onto a side street, and Meghan kept her distance; she did not want them to know she was on their tail. She waited fifteen seconds, and then proceeded, charging ahead as quickly as she could without giving herself away.

When she turned the corner, she sighed; she had lost sight of Bonnie and the strange man, and they were nowhere to be found.

"Who is she with?" she thought to herself as she surveyed the empty streets of Sandy Bay. "And what's going on?"

18

M eghan looked left and looked right, craning her neck as she tried to see where Bonnie and the strange man had wandered off to. Who was Bonnie meeting with, and why were they embracing? Meghan did not know, but she had a gut feeling that she *needed* to find out.

After ten minutes of searching, she gasped as she looked down at her watch. Her lunch break was nearly over, and she turned on her heel and rushed over to Big Catch. James was in the lobby when she arrived, and he greeted her with a grin. "Let's plan that date night."

She nodded, but as he led her to a table and pulled out several brochures, she started to worry about the trip. Did she have the stamina or courage to survive a deep-sea fishing expedition? She was not sure.

"And this is our Shark Tale package," he told her as he pushed a folder across the table. "In this excursion, we sail out to the middle of ocean and fish for sharks. We've caught big ones on this trip; it's a bit intense, but the look on

Jack's face when he catches his first shark will be worth it, I promise you."

She shuddered. "I don't know if I can handle sharks," she politely declined. "Do you have anything less... involved?"

He laughed. "Of course," he assured her. "What about our Coastal Cruise?"

"That sounds nice," she admitted. "Tell me more?"

"It's a quiet boat ride down the coast," he laughed. "Very self-explanatory. Guests have the option of doing a little light fishing, but most of the time is spent inside of the boat. This is the perfect package for guests who tend to be a little seasick or nervous about being in the open water."

Her face brightened. "I think that's the perfect package for me. How did you come up with that one? It doesn't sound quite as adventurous as the rest of your offerings."

His face darkened. "Bonnie."

She raised an eyebrow. "Huh?"

James' face darkened. "Bonnie hated the open water," he complained as he gathered the brochures and placed them back in their respective folders. "She always whined to Anthony about the trips we offered, and eventually, he demanded we add one for our more delicate guests. No offense."

She smiled. "None taken."

"Anyway, we designed this tour for *her*, and of course, she never bothered going on it. Bonnie hated the business and business dealings. She honestly would have been a good politician's wife—she's more of the fancy type than the adventure company type. It's a shame she won't get to live out her dream..."

Meghan pursed her lips. "What was it like to work with Anthony?"

James smiled. "He was a great face for our business," he told her. "Quite literally, in fact; his good looks helped us snag so many deals, and he certainly had a way with people. I did more of the behind-the-scenes work. I worked on the daily operations of the business, and this arrangement worked for us."

"I'm sure it's been hard to lose your friend," she offered. "I'm sorry. Were you at the town hall meeting on the night he died?"

James ignored her question. "Anthony was obsessed with the limelight," he continued. "But most people didn't realize he was a big loner; he hated spending too much time with people, and he always needed his space and quiet time."

She stared at him. "James?"

"I was working when Anthony was killed," James mumbled. "Working behind the scenes, as always."

She pursed her lips. "Who did it, James?" she asked softly. "Do you know who did it?"

James looked into her eyes, a cloudy look on his face. "Anthony had a lot of enemies," he murmured. "He hurt a lot of people, Meghan. He made a lot of promises to a lot of people. But he wasn't a bad guy. He was a broken man. It's like that saying goes: hurt people, hurt people. That's what Anthony was. He was hurting."

"So, who hurt *him?*"

His face fell. "I'm sure someone came for payback," he stated matter-of-factly. "Someone he hurt or cheated. But he hurt and cheated many people. Who knows if we'll ever know who killed him?"

Just then, the receptionist waved James over. "Boss? Someone is here to see you."

"Excuse me."

James rose from his seat and walked over to the reception desk. "Can I help you?"

A burly man with a thick beard greeted him. "Just needed to turn in my locker key and uniform," he told James. "And I wanted to pay my respects to Anthony. It's a shame that he is gone, and with no funeral, I felt like coming by. The shop was as close as I could get to paying respects."

James nodded. "That's very kind of you," Meghan heard him reply.

The man started crying. "Anthony was one of a kind," he sighed, wiping his eyes. "He was a good man, and a good boss. I'll always think highly of him."

"I know you will," James smiled weakly. "Thanks for stopping by. It was nice of you to pop in."

"Of course," the man told James. "I didn't know what else to do."

The two men hugged, and then the man left. James returned to the table; his face drawn.

"What was that all about?" Meghan asked. "Who was that man?"

James scowled. "He was a former employee," he told Meghan. "Business has been down, and we've had to make some difficult layoffs. Barry had worked for us for five years. He has a family and three little kids, and we had to let him go."

Her dark eyes grew large. "Why? What's going on with your business?"

James shook his head. "I can't quite put my finger on it," he admitted. "But something has been off. Funds have been disappearing, and with no paper trail, it's been hard to figure out the issue."

"Anthony?" she whispered, and he shrugged.

"I don't know," he glowered. "But whatever happened, it's now affecting people's lives. It really stinks."

"I'm sorry," she told him. "I'm really sorry for all you've been through."

"Me too," he smiled. "Hard times help you remember the important things, though. Family, friends, and making good memories are what matters. Let's finish your paperwork and get you ready for that romantic trip with your man. What do you say?"

Ten minutes later, Meghan walked out of the Big Catch office, her mind abuzz with questions. Who had taken funds from the shop? Had Anthony Diggs embezzled money from his own business? Could James be responsible? She was not sure, but as she headed back toward the bakery, she could not stop thinking about the burly man who had cried over Anthony. Who *was* Anthony Diggs, really? Did anyone in town know the real Anthony, or had he swindled every single person he knew?

She crossed the street, and her face brightened, seeing a familiar face walking toward her.

"Hey," she greeted warmly. "It's so good to see you."

"I've been looking for you. We *need* to talk."

19

Meghan blinked as Erin Rogers hurried over to her. "We need to talk?" she asked, worried that Erin was upset with her. "Is everything okay?"

Erin smiled, and Meghan felt relief. "Of course it's okay," she assured her. "I just wanted to go over a few more notes about the dessert tasting."

"Ahhhh," Meghan breathed. "We can certainly do that, Erin. When are you free?"

Erin shrugged. "Does now work? I was just stretching my legs during my lunch break. We could walk and talk?"

Meghan nodded. She needed to get back to the bakery, but technically, this *was* a business meeting. She could spare another hour.

"Sure," she told Erin. "Let's walk and talk."

They made their way to the beach, both women shivering as the frigid ocean breeze hit their faces. "I love it over here," Erin murmured as she opened her arms and inhaled the salty air. "I sometimes meet my fiance here on my lunch breaks. I love it when we walk along the shore, arm in arm."

Meghan looked out over the dark waters of the Pacific

Ocean. "I never get tired of it," she declared. "I grew up in Texas, but now, after living in Los Angeles and Sandy Bay, I could never be landlocked again."

"You're so lucky to have lived in Los Angeles," Erin told her, gathering up her curls and tying them back into a low ponytail. "I always wanted to try my hand at acting or modeling, but I've only ever lived in Sandy Bay. When I was a teenager, I dreamed of moving to Hollywood and making it big! Can you imagine what it's like to be a famous actress? You would make so much money, and you would never have to worry about anything."

Meghan giggled. "Actresses and models have their demons. Trust me. And the acting and modeling scene in Los Angeles isn't all it's cracked up to be," she promised, thinking back to the long days of auditions, barely being able to pay her rent, and the nasty comments about her appearance or performances from arrogant directors and assistants. "Sandy Bay is so relaxed and quiet. It's the perfect place for me."

Erin stared out at the sea. "It's not so quiet anymore," she muttered, trudging through the sand. "What do you think about Anthony Diggs' murder? Isn't it crazy?"

Meghan shook her head. "I didn't know him very well," she told her. "It is sad, though. I feel bad for his wife."

Erin's face darkened. "I think she did it," she stated as Meghan turned to stare at her. "And so does everyone I know. Bonnie Diggs has always thought she was too good for this town, and killing Anthony was her ticket out."

"You really think so?"

"I do," Erin told her. "My colleagues think it was Marty, that guy at the radio station; apparently Marty and Anthony had some beef over money. But the more we talked about it, the more we thought Bonnie had something to do with it all. Who knows, Meghan? Maybe Bonnie and Marty are having some sort of affair and they *both* killed him."

"That could be," Meghan agreed, thinking of the mystery man she had seen with Bonnie. "Do you know Bonnie well?"

"No one does," Erin sniffed. "She's haughty and stiff, and she doesn't mingle with us Sandy Bay folks anymore. I guess her days of modeling in Paris made her too special to connect with us normal people."

Meghan detected a hint of jealousy in Erin's voice. "I think the police will get to the bottom of it all," she finally sighed. "Sooner than later, I hope…"

Erin changed the subject. "How did you like wedding planning?" She asked Meghan. "Most people say it's a bother, but I've really enjoyed it."

Meghan saw the excitement in her eyes. "You will make a lovely bride," she complimented Erin. "All of us gals at the bakery are really looking forward to your big day."

Erin beamed. "I'm so fortunate to be marrying my Prince Charming," she cooed. "He is such a wonderful, genuine person. He's always been laid back and low key; he prefers to be behind the scenes, so I don't know how much attention he'll be able to stand on our wedding day, but I hope it is the best day of his life."

Meghan nodded. "You both will definitely be in the lime-light on your wedding day," she promised Erin. "I remember when Jack and I got married, we felt like celebrities; everyone wanted to take our picture and make sure we were happy and comfortable. It was such a fun day."

"I can't wait," Erin exclaimed. "We will get married and live happily ever after."

"I love how excited you are about your big day," Meghan told her.

"You have no idea," Erin sighed, looking down at her watch. "Oh, Meghan, I am so sorry, but I have to get back to work."

They turned to walk back toward town. As they passed

Big Catch, James Kittle stuck his head out the front door and waved at them. He blew a kiss toward Erin, and she blushed.

"Love you, hon!" she called out, blowing a kiss back at him.

James went back inside, and Erin grinned. "He is such a doll," she gushed as they crossed the street. "Isn't he handsome? He will make such a darling groom. I love James Kittle with all of my heart!"

20

M eghan pulled her phone out of her pocket and dialed Trudy's number.

"Where are you?" Trudy squawked as Meghan turned back toward town. "You told us you would be back an hour ago."

"Sorry," she apologized, quickening her pace as she realized it was nearly two in the afternoon. "I got caught up talking with Erin Rogers."

"Did she have any more notes about her wedding?" Trudy asked. "She emailed the bakery and mentioned that she had some more suggestions, but she did not specify exactly what she wanted."

Meghan gulped. "We didn't get around to talking about that," she admitted. "But we did chat about James. Did you know Erin is his fiancée? I had no idea. They are such a cute couple. She really loves him."

"James Kittle and Erin Rogers?" Trudy asked. "Really? They just seem so different."

Meghan shrugged. "I guess what they say is true: opposites attract."

"That James Kittle is a good-looking fellow," Trudy told her. "His father and I went to school together, and John Kittle was the star of the baseball team. James was even more talented; they always wrote about him in the local papers. He loved to wrestle, though; he wasn't into baseball like his father."

"James Kittle can wrestle?" Meghan asked, feeling her stomach sink.

"Like a champion," Trudy went on. "He won the state championship three years in a row."

Meghan swallowed, feeling a cold sweat come over her. Anthony Diggs had been strangled, she remembered. James Kittle was a talented wrestler. Was there a connection?

As she pondered this possibility, she saw a flash of red out of the corner of her eye. It was Bonnie Diggs. She was several yards ahead of Meghan, still walking with the mysterious man.

"Who is she with?" Meghan wondered as she pumped her arms vigorously, trying to catch up to Bonnie and the man. "And what are they doing together?"

Meghan followed closely behind as Bonnie and the man walked arm-in-arm through the streets of Sandy Bay. She watched as they laughed and kidded with each other, stopping to joke and play every few minutes.

"Are they a couple?" she thought as she saw Bonnie lean over and give the man a kiss on the cheek. "They certainly look like they are together. What is going on here?"

Bonnie and the man turned left, and Meghan saw them take off toward the beach. She groaned, knowing there wasn't much cover down by the beach; there were no trees and very few large rocks, and she would have few places to hide as she followed them.

She frowned, frustrated that she could no longer track

them. She felt her phone buzz and pulled it out of her pocket. Trudy was calling her back.

"Hey," she greeted her. "Sorry, I'm on my way."

"Don't come back," Trudy cautioned her. "Not until you stop by the market. We're out of eggs, and we need you to grab some on your way back."

Meghan raised an eyebrow. "Out of eggs?"

"It's Pamela," Trudy whispered to her. "It's the inventory stuff. She messed up again, Meghan. We're out of eggs, and we'll be out of butter soon. It's a mess."

Meghan groaned. "Can you put Pamela on the phone?"

She heard Trudy pass the phone to Pamela. "What's going on?"

"I'm sorry," Pamela told her quietly. "I should have double and triple checked the grocery order. I messed up."

Meghan felt annoyed as she heard the break in Pamela's voice. Pamela had been careless over the last few days, and Meghan was tired of having to chide her for simple mistakes.

"You asked for more responsibilities," Meghan said softly. "And I gave them to you. Trudy has made every effort to help you learn the role of a manager. What's the problem, Pamela? Are you not paying attention to Trudy? Are you blowing her off when she is trying to teach you? I don't understand."

"I don't know," Pamela moaned. "I'm sorry, Meghan. I'll do better. I've been thinking about school and about Paul—"

"Who is Paul?" Meghan asked.

"My boyfriend!"

Meghan sighed. "This again?" she asked the teenager. "Look, Pamela, the last time you had a boyfriend, your performance at work was poor. It was a hard time for all of us, and I really wish you would focus your energy on the important things, like school, your sports, friends, and work."

"That's what my mom said," Pamela muttered. "I'll do

better, okay? I'm sorry, Meghan. I'll show you I can make it all work."

"Put Trudy back on the phone, please," Meghan asked.

Trudy took the phone back from Pamela. "That girl," she muttered as Meghan shook her head.

"I'll get the eggs and some more butter," Meghan assured her. "Anything else we are coming up short on?"

"Let me check."

Meghan heard her walk into the refrigerator. "Probably more brown sugar, coconut flour, vegetable oil, and bananas," Trudy told her. "She really didn't do any of the inventory checks I asked her to do…"

"I'll talk to her," Meghan promised. "After I get back from the grocery store."

They hung up the phone, and Meghan walked quickly to the market. She was irritated with Pamela; why couldn't the girl just do her job without complication? Meghan tried to empathize with her; Pamela worked a lot, did several sports, and made perfect grades. Maybe she was just letting off some steam with this new boyfriend. Meghan wasn't sure, but she hoped things wouldn't get as bad as they did when Pamela was dating Roberto, the son of the local funeral home director.

At the market, Meghan was pleased to find that things had mostly gotten back to normal. The papers in the news-stands still had articles about Anthony, but the atmosphere in the store was peaceful. Crowds of women weren't huddled around the perimeter of the store, and Meghan was able to shop in peace.

She turned down the dairy aisle and bumped into some-one, almost losing her footing as the breath was knocked out of her by the collision.

"Sorry," she groaned, her dark eyes growing huge when she realized she had run right into Bonnie Diggs.

Bonnie narrowed her green eyes at Meghan. "What is your problem?" she asked, her face drawn and eyes flashing with anger. "Why have you been stalking me? I've seen you following me around town today, and I want you to help me understand why you think you can watch me?"

Meghan's jaw dropped. "I... I..."

Bonnie raised her eyebrows. "You what? What is your problem? Why are you following me? Haven't I been through enough over the last few weeks? I don't understand what your problem is."

Meghan stared at her. "I don't know what to say," she offered meekly. "I'm sorry."

Bonnie scowled, her dainty features contorting and her pretty face filling with rage. "Sorry? Sorry isn't going to do it; I have been through the worst of the worst, and having some busybody small town girl follow me is simply too much. You need to cut it out, or I will call the police."

A uniformed store attendant walked over. "Is everything okay, ladies?"

Bonnie vigorously shook her head. "It is not okay," she declared, staring straight at Meghan. "This woman is harassing me."

The store attendant looked at Meghan. "Ma'am?"

"That's not true," Meghan insisted. "I accidentally ran into her. It was a mistake. I turned into the dairy aisle to grab some eggs and bumped into her. I didn't mean it."

Bonnie glowered at her. "She's lying," she insisted. "This woman has been stalking me, and I want her removed from the store."

The attendant looked at Meghan. "Can you leave her alone, please?"

Meghan nodded. "Of course."

"Thank you."

The attendant turned to Bonnie. "If she bothers you again, please come up front and we will take care of it."

He walked away, and Bonnie and Meghan were left to themselves. Bonnie held her head high. "You heard him. Leave me alone."

Meghan frowned. "Maybe if you acted like a widow, I wouldn't be wondering about you…"

Bonnie's eyes widened. "What did you just say?"

Overcome with frustration, Meghan balled her hands into fists. "You aren't carrying yourself like a widow," she explained in a strained voice. "You're running around town acting lovey dovey with a man. Who is he, Bonnie? Did Anthony know about him?"

Bonnie narrowed her eyes. "You don't know anything about me," she whispered to Meghan. "And maybe if you had just asked politely, instead of making assumptions, I would feel more inclined to share with you."

Meghan stared at her. "What kind of trouble are you in, Bonnie?" she asked quietly. "What is going on? Who is that man?"

Bonnie gave a cynical laugh. "Do you really want to know? Okay, then. That man? He's my brother, Meghan. My *brother.*"

21

The color drained from Meghan's face. "Your brother?" she whispered as she felt her heart sink. "That man is your *brother?*"

Bonnie nodded. "He came up from Encinitas to be with me."

Meghan hung her head. "I don't even know what to say," she admitted, feeling nauseated as she thought of the ways she had judged Bonnie. "I'm so sorry."

Bonnie's face broke into a smile. "You're pretty embarrassed, aren't you? Your face is the color of a tomato."

Meghan bit her lip. "I am so humiliated," she whispered as she gathered her face in her hands. "Bonnie, please forgive me. I can't believe I made those assumptions and made such a scene..."

Bonnie awkwardly patted her shoulder. "It happens to the best of us," she told Meghan. "I'm sorry I made a big deal about it here in public. You're been one of the few people in Sandy Bay to be kind to me, and I guess I was just hurt that you changed your tune and were coming after me during this difficult time."

Meghan nodded. "Why don't we go outside and talk?"

They left the store and sat outside on a wooden bench. "So... your brother…"

"He's the greatest," Bonnie smiled. "Bryant is ten years older than me, so we didn't really grow up together, but as adults, we've become quite close. He's an attorney, and when I lived in Paris, he managed my affairs and served as my manager. He has a wife and kids now, so we don't get to see each other often, but he flew up here to be with me when he found out about Anthony."

"You're lucky to have such a supportive family," Meghan sighed. "Bryant sounds like a wonderful person."

"He's dependable and decent," Bonnie agreed. "I'm thankful his love is something I can always rely on, and I'm thankful he is here to help me sort through all the complex details of Anthony's affairs."

Meghan's face darkened. "His... affairs?"

Bonnie frowned. "His *legal* affairs," she elaborated, crossing her arms over her chest. "Though I know about the other affairs," she added softly. "I'm not a fool."

Meghan looked down at her shoes. "I'm sorry," she offered, but Bonnie shook her head.

"That's all anyone says to me anymore," she laughed darkly. "People keep telling me they are sorry. What are they sorry for, though? Are they sorry my husband is dead? Are they sorry that he squandered most of our fortune, and that his life insurance money is all I will have left? Are they sorry Anthony was a crook and a cheater, and that I spent so much time in California with my parents because he was off with his girlfriends?"

Meghan looked Bonnie in the eyes. "I think they're sorry about all of it," she breathed. "You've been through so much, Bonnie, and I can only imagine people just feel terrible about what you've had to go through."

Bonnie shivered. "They haven't made a good show of feeling terrible for me," she complained. "You're the only one who has been kind to me, and you just tried to publicly humiliate me."

Meghan's face burned with shame. "I'm sorry."

"There you go again," Bonnie chuckled. "Saying that you are sorry. I need to get out of this town. I can't take another minute of people feeling sorry for me or laughing behind my back about all the ways my husband did me wrong."

"Tell me more about Anthony," Meghan said quietly. "The parts of him you loved…"

Bonnie's eyes grew dreamy. "The parts I loved? Oh, Meghan. Anthony was a dreamer. He was a visionary. He was handsome and charming, and people adored him. He was fun and well-liked, and it felt like a privilege to be with him."

"He sounds like the kind of person people like to be around," Meghan added.

"Oh, for sure," Bonnie agreed. "People loved to be around Anthony. He would have loved being mayor. He was so excited about his candidacy, and I know he would have made such a splash at that town hall that night…"

She saw a flash of despair in Bonnie's face. "Where were you that night?" she murmured. "Were you the one who found him?"

"I saw him briefly in the back room before it started," she told Meghan. "He was in good spirits, drinking tea and joking around."

"Did anything seem off?"

Bonnie shook her head. "He seemed like the Anthony everyone knew and loved. Look, Meghan, I loved my husband. Despite all his indiscretions, we were married. We shared a life together. That just doesn't get erased because of difficult times. My life has been so closely intertwined with his for over a decade. I don't know what I am going to do now…"

Meghan saw the sadness in her green eyes. "I'm sorry," she said again, and this time, Bonnie smiled.

"Enough with that," she urged Meghan. "If I hear one more person tell me they are sorry, I am going to strangle someone."

Meghan's jaw dropped. "That was a bad joke," Bonnie apologized. "But I am the widow, here. If I want to make a joke in bad taste, I think I get a free pass, given the circumstances, don't you?"

Meghan smiled. "I think you do."

Bonnie chuckled. "I was so angry with you back there in the supermarket," she commented. "But I've liked talking with you out here. It's nice to have someone to talk to, especially with everything going on."

Meghan blinked. Bonnie's voice was sincere, and the look in her eyes was of genuine appreciation. Perhaps she had misjudged Bonnie, jumping too quickly to conclusions that Bonnie had something to do with her husband's death. Overcome with guilt, she extended a hand to Bonnie. "Friends? I would love to hear all about your adventures in Paris, and I think your style is impeccable. Can we be friends, Bonnie?"

Bonnie nodded. "Only if you promise to never cause a scene with me in the supermarket ever again."

"It's a deal."

The ladies finished their conversation, and Meghan turned to head back to Truly Sweet. As she walked, she groaned when she realized she did not have the eggs or other groceries Trudy asked for. She begrudgingly turned back around and went into the supermarket.

She spotted Bonnie from afar. She was happy that they had resolved their issues; Bonnie seemed like a nice, witty woman, and Meghan was happy to have a new friend. She felt bad for having suspected the widow, and as she approached her, she thought of inviting Bonnie over to the bakery for tea later.

Bonnie was conversing with another shopper, a pretty young woman with long black hair pulled back into two plaits. As Meghan neared them, she realized the conversation was heated; Bonnie's face was drawn, and she was shaking a fist at the other woman.

"Don't you dare talk to me about my husband," she warned at the black-haired woman, who was smirking at her. "You have no right to talk about Mr. Diggs that way."

"Anthony and I knew each other quite well," the woman countered.

Was this one of Anthony's mistresses? Meghan saw the rage in Bonnie's eyes. Should she step in?

"Anthony never talked about you," the woman declared, and Bonnie's jaw dropped. "He never spoke a word about his sad, lonely, old wife."

Bonnie lunged for the woman, grabbing her by one of her long braids and tugging hard. "You will not talk about my late husband like that," she ordered as the woman screeched in pain.

"Help me! She's crazy. She's attacking me!" the woman cried out, and Bonnie quickly let go.

Meghan backed away slowly, and then turned on her heel, hurrying out of the supermarket. What had she just witnessed? She had not imagined the elegant, refined Bonnie Diggs could attack someone in a jealous rage, but she had just seen it happen in public. What was Bonnie capable of in *private*? Could a jealous Bonnie have attacked her husband, or worse, killed him? Meghan had a bad feeling, and as she darted back to the bakery, she could not shake the idea that Bonnie was hiding something.

The next morning, Meghan woke up early, excited about her date with Jack that afternoon. They were booked for the coastal cruise, and Meghan had called Big Catch and secretly upgraded the trip to include an hour of deep sea fishing, knowing Jack would love it. It was the perfect combination of a romantic date and an adventure date, and she could not wait for some quality time alone with her husband.

When she went into the kitchen to make breakfast, she found Sarah standing over the stove, dressed in her bathrobe and humming as she flipped bacon. "That smells great," she complimented as she went to the refrigerator and retrieved a carton of almond milk. "Thanks for making breakfast, Sarah."

"My pleasure," Sarah smiled. "I wanted to make all the meals for us today; I know you've had a busy week, and I want to help. You should see what I'm cooking up for a late lunch; I was thinking halibut with a lemon butter sauce would be lovely. Jack loves halibut."

"That sounds great," Meghan agreed. "But Jack and I will be out, remember?"

Sarah's face fell. "Oh," she replied softly. "That's right. I forgot you two have a date planned for this afternoon. I guess I'll just order takeout or something. There is no point in cooking a fancy meal if it's only for one person."

Meghan saw the hurt in her eyes. "What are you going to do today?" she asked her mother-in-law. "There's a great movie playing at the theater downtown. Maybe you could check it out?"

"Seeing a movie alone is so pitiful," Sarah clucked. "I'll just hang out here, I suppose…"

Meghan's heart sank. She knew Sarah hated being alone, but she needed to have a date night with her husband. She wondered if she could compromise; Sarah had been a huge help around the house lately, and Meghan had started to really enjoy her company.

"Why don't we go for a walk together?" Meghan asked kindly. "We can spend some time hanging out, just the two of us."

Sarah sighed. "I don't know."

"Come on," Meghan urged her. "It's a beautiful day, the sun is shining, and it isn't too cold. We can take the dogs over to the beach and have some mother-daughter time."

Sarah's face lit up. "Mother-daughter time?"

Meghan grinned. "You are my mother now," she began. "And you don't have any daughters. I think we should get to know each other even better, and a walk would be a great start."

Sarah beamed. "I'll finish making breakfast and we can go," she told her. "What a lovely idea."

An hour later, Meghan, Sarah, and the three dogs were walking along the snowy, sandy shores at the local beach. It was unusually warm for a winter day in the Pacific Northwest, and Meghan was relieved to only have to wear a sweat-shirt instead of her large, puffy winter coat.

"This sunshine is good for my soul," she commented as she unclipped the dogs from their leashes and let them run free. "The winter is so hard for me; Jack jokes that I'm like a plant, in need of constant sunshine."

"You won't get that around here," Sarah cautioned her. "Winters are hard for me, too. Jack's father takes me to Phoenix and Sedona for a few weeks each winter, and that helps my mood a lot. Maybe you two should start a tradition of a warm-weather winter vacation."

Meghan nodded. "That's a great idea," she agreed. "We'll have to look into it."

Sarah glanced at her. "Maybe we could make it a family vacation?" she asked hopefully. "Once a year, or every other year?"

"I would like that," Meghan answered honestly. "Spending time with family is one of the most important things there is."

Sarah smiled, and Meghan's heart warmed. She was glad that they had grown closer, and she felt relieved that they were finally getting along. She liked Sarah; her mother-in-law was motherly and warm, unlike her own mother, and now that they had resolved their tensions, it was fun having her around the house.

"I've loved being here," Sarah told her as they strolled along the shoreline. "You and Jack have really made me feel welcome."

"I'm so glad," Meghan told her, a smile on her face. "I was just thinking about how much fun it's been to have you at our home. I'm glad we can get along and have fun together."

Fiesta ran over to them, and Sarah picked the dog up and gave her a kiss on the forehead. "I've even warmed up to these dogs," she commented as Fiesta licked her face. "I never imagined I could love a little dog like this, but now, I want to get one of my own."

"Puppies are difficult to have in the house," Meghan warned her. "They take a lot of work and care. Can I make a recommendation?"

"Of course."

"Adopt a grown dog from the shelter," she suggested as Sarah scratched Fiesta behind the ears. "Grown dogs have usually been trained, and it's much less of a hassle to integrate them into the house."

"I think Jack's father would prefer an older dog, anyway," Sarah agreed. "He wouldn't do well with a loud, yippy dog."

Meghan smiled. "If you need any advice about dogs, feel free to call me anytime," she promised her mother-in-law. "I love them so much, and I am always happy to help."

Sarah reached out and gave Meghan's arm a squeeze. "And if you ever need any advice about Jack, my door is always open," she told her sweetly. "I know you two are married now, and you probably don't need his mother interfering, but I know my son well. I know his likes and dislikes, for the most part, and I know how his father is. If there is anything you need, or my son gives you trouble, I want you to call me."

Meghan was touched by this statement; Sarah's voice was earnest, and she could tell her mother-in-law truly wanted the best for her. "I will," she told her as they linked elbows, walking arm-in-arm. "I will."

As they strolled, they saw a woman approaching them. She was dressed in a knee-length lilac coat and matching boots, her curly hair pulled back into a messy braid. Meghan recognized her as she drew nearer; it was Erin Rogers, and she was waving at them.

"Hi, Erin," Meghan greeted her. "That's one of my

136

customers," she whispered to Sarah. "She's placed a massive order with us for her wedding; it's a big deal."

"That's lovely," Sarah cooed as Erin smiled at them. "Hello, there. I'm Meghan's mother-in-law."

"Nice to meet you," Erin grinned. "Isn't it a gorgeous day? I can't believe how warm it is. I hope it's this warm on my wedding day; I want to do some photos outdoors, and I can't do that in a blizzard."

Meghan shrugged. "Your wedding photos will be spectacular inside or outside," she assured her. "What are you up to today?"

"The usual, though James tells me you and Jack have some big plans later today."

"That's right," Meghan confirmed. "Jack and I are so excited; we're going out on the boat this evening for our date night."

"What a treat," Erin cried. "I'm so excited for you. Do you have everything you need? Big Catch provides the fishing gear, but passengers have to bring a GPS. I didn't know if you knew that or not; last time we had a couple out for this cruise, they didn't know, and the boat didn't have a GPS. They were lost for ten hours, and the coast guard had to rescue them."

"Oh my," Meghan blinked. "I didn't see that in the paperwork. I'll have to go out and get one today."

"Don't forget it," Erin urged her. "It's so important."

Sarah caught sight of Erin's engagement ring. "That's so pretty," she complimented as Erin wiggled her fingers, clearly enjoying the attention. "Do you have all of your wedding plans made, yet?"

"Not quite," Erin admitted. "We are still finalizing the flowers and the music for the reception. I really want a band, but James thinks having a DJ would be cooler."

"What flowers are you thinking of?" Sarah asked.

"Peonies, of course," Erin replied. "Coral peonies would be so pretty. I also like ranunculus, though; they look like little scoops of ice cream, and they've always been my favorite."

Sarah pursed her lips. "Can't you do both?" she asked. "Tell your florist to incorporate both flowers; soft yellow ranunculus would set off coral peonies so nicely, and you could even add a bit of baby's breath or some red roses to balance out the color palette."

Erin's face brightened. "That's a marvelous idea," she praised Sarah. "You have nice taste."

"My garden at home is filled with roses in the summer," Sarah smiled dreamily. "I think red roses make any bouquet or arrangement come to life."

Erin turned to Meghan. "Could you make some edible little red roses to put on top of the cakes?"

"Of course," Meghan told her. "We can do anything you'd like, within reason, and I think edible roses are certainly within reason for your wedding."

Erin's smile widened. "These are such great ideas," she told them as she tucked a loose ringlet behind her ear. "What a wonderful surprise it was running into you both. I have to go now, but Meghan, I'll be in touch about the cakes."

Sarah and Meghan returned home and found Jack waiting for them in the living room. He was dressed in a navy blue suit and tan dress shoes. Meghan raised an eyebrow. "Babe? What are you doing? Why are you dressed up so nicely?"

Jack stared at her. "It's our date night, remember?"

She laughed. "We're going fishing, honey. I added on a fishing package to our trip. Not to a ball or a business meeting."

Jack shook his head. "We haven't had a nice night out together in a long time," he protested. "And this will be romantic. I don't care if my suit gets wet or slimy; my wife deserves to see me at my best."

"That is so romantic," Sarah gushed, but Meghan bit her lip. "Babe, I'm wearing leggings, a vest, and a sweater," she told him. "Are you sure you want to go dressed in a suit?"

He stood his ground. "Absolutely," he declared. "And I won't regret it one bit."

23

"You two are good to go," James grinned as he walked them to the boat, a small, but sturdy vessel that was approximately as long and wide as the dining room of the bakery. "The sea is calm today, and you two should have plenty of fun out there."

Meghan looked at him in alarm. "You aren't coming with us?"

James shook his head. "We have the route programmed into the boat's system," he told her. "You two will get on the boat, sail for two or so hours, and then the boat will steer itself back to us. It's like autopilot on an airplane."

"And if there's an emergency?" she fretted. "Then what?"

James smiled reassuringly. "We've never had a problem," he told her. "But if something comes up, the ship is equipped with emergency gear, as well as a telephone and walkie talkies. You'll only be a few yards offshore, and it would be easy for us to get to you if anything went wrong."

Jack smiled. "Meghan, relax. This will be fun."

"That's the spirit," James cheered. "Don't forget to keep your life jackets close. We have a drone system that's keeping watch over the boat, so when it's time to come in, we'll be waiting here for you at the dock."

Meghan gulped. "Are you sure this is safe?"

"As long as you have your life jackets and a GPS, nothing bad can happen."

Her stomach sank. "The GPS," she groaned. "Erin told me that we would need one, and I forgot to pick one up."

James laughed. "That's why we keep them in stock back at the shop. Why don't you go grab it, Meghan, and I will help Jack load the gear onto the boat?"

"Okay," she said, and she turned to walk up the beach and over to Big Catch.

As she neared the shop, she spotted Bryant, Bonnie's older brother. He stormed out of the shop, his face angry, and she stepped back so he wouldn't walk right into her.

"Excuse me," he grumbled as he strode away mumbling.

Meghan craned her neck, trying to hear what he was saying. He was muttering something about "malicious people", and she wondered who he was referring to. She saw him walk away, pumping his arms vigorously as he disappeared off into the night.

She walked into Big Catch, and James walked in behind her. "I thought you were helping Jack load the boat," she said as she registered the look on his face. The shop was quiet; none of the other employees were there, and Meghan wondered where they were. "Did you see the guy who just left? He practically ran me over as I was coming in. Do you know him? Bonnie's brother?"

James sighed. "I know him," he told her as he walked over to his desk and put his head down. "Trust me, I know him."

She walked over to him, a confused look on her face. "What's wrong?"

He straightened up and turned to the shelves behind the desk. "You need the GPS," he muttered as he looked up and down the shelves. "Sorry, Meghan. I'll find it and get you out the door in a jiff."

She crossed her arms over her chest, her head cocked to the side. "What's wrong, James?" she repeated as he fumbled with a storage box.

His shoulders slumped. "It's nothing," he promised her.

"Clearly something is wrong," she observed, and he turned back to her.

"It's Bonnie and her brother," he muttered, staring down at his boots, shame filling his face. "They want to buy the shop from me."

She stared at him. "Like... buy you out?"

"Exactly."

She bit her lip. "Is that a bad thing?" she asked. "Have they made a good offer? You *are* getting married soon. Wouldn't it be nice to have some extra cash on hand? You could put it toward your wedding or even start a new business. Something Anthony didn't have a part in."

"That's what they suggested," he groaned. "But I don't know if I *want* that, Meghan. This business has been my passion and dream. I've put so much into it, and my team has been through so much. I don't know if I want to sell and start over."

She watched as his lips began to tremble. "Are you okay?"

"I'm not okay," he hissed as he balled his hands into fists. "Anthony almost ruined this business; I have so much credit card debt and issues from trying to bail us out over and over and over again. Debt collectors have been coming around here, and a guy at the bank mentioned my work truck getting repossessed if I don't pay the balance on it by Monday."

"Then let his wife take care of it," she suggested. "Let her buy the business, and it won't be your problem anymore. Isn't that the easiest solution to your problems?"

He tried not to cry. "I don't know if it'll fix things," he explained quietly. "Anthony dug us into a hole, and I don't know if Bonnie's money will get us out. Meghan, you have no idea how bad the finances have been around here. Bonnie has made some offers, but I know Anthony ruined *her* too. She doesn't have a pile of money lying around, and it's going to take a pile of money to fix this. I've had to postpone my wedding *twice* because of my credit card debt. It's not fair. It's not fair that I had to clean up his messes, and now, my fiance is going to suffer because of it *again*."

"That must be so hard," Meghan sympathized. "What do you think you're going to do?"

"I don't know," he lamented. "But I need to do something, or I'll lose everything."

"What are you talking about?"

James' face crumbled. "The books, Meghan…"

She stared at him. "The books?"

"The police have already started talking to our employees," he muttered, closing his eyes and taking a long breath. "I have an appointment to talk with them tomorrow morning. They're on to me."

She raised an eyebrow. "On to you? I don't understand. I thought Anthony was the mastermind of everything that went wrong."

James' chin began to tremble. "I took some money from the business," he confessed. "Not a lot, but enough to pay off some of my debt and to pay for my wedding. I just wanted to settle up my personal debts—debts that exist because of Anthony's mistakes—before moving on to saving the shop. It was wrong, and I shouldn't have done it, but I did. Now, I'm going to lose everything. What if they take me to jail?"

"You've already lost everything."

They turned around to see Erin Rogers step out of the shadows. She was dressed in black leggings, a long black sweatshirt, and had a gray scarf draped around her neck. "You're a fool, James. You let Anthony Diggs walk all over you for years, and now, you're going to let his widow buy you out for less than what you deserve? Typical."

James' eyes widened. "Honey? What are you doing here? I thought you were going to a movie?"

Erin shook her head. Meghan gasped when she realized Erin was holding a small, shiny gun in her left hand. "I regret agreeing to marry you," she spat as she held the gun to James' forehead. "You lack ambition and charisma, and you just keep embarrassing yourself as you let people walk all over you. And now, you're baring your soul to her? Why did you have to run your mouth, James? Now it's too late…"

James held up his hands in shock. "Babe? What is going on? Is this some kind of joke?"

Erin gestured at Meghan. "I heard you two talking," she muttered as the hand holding the gun began to shake. "You told her too much, James. Why would you do that? Trust someone who isn't your fiancée. What a foolish move…"

She pivoted to face Meghan and fired the gun. Meghan screamed, ducking beneath a reclaimed wood table and covering her head.

"I should have practiced at the shooting range," Erin groaned, turning back to her fiance. "You shouldn't have spilled the beans, James."

"Erin, come on, stop playing around," he begged her. "This isn't funny."

She stared into his eyes. "I'm not laughing," she said flatly before pulling the trigger and shooting him in the chest.

Meghan let out a wail as she heard James' body slump to the ground. She was in shock, but she quickly sprung into action, leaping around the side of the table and darting toward the front door.

"Where do you think you are going?" Erin called out as she followed Meghan, trapping her in a corner.

"Why are you doing this?" Meghan screamed, holding her arms up to shield her face. "Erin, what is going on? Why are you attacking us?"

Erin stepped closer to Meghan, who was now backed up against a corner. There was nowhere for her to hide, and both women knew it.

"Your cakes were great, you know," she told Meghan as she adjusted the gun and steadied it in her hand. "I was really looking forward to your desserts. If my idiot fiance had kept his mouth shut, I would be enjoying them at our wedding. Unfortunately though, it appears there won't be a wedding. Or you, for that matter."

Meghan closed her eyes. She thought of Jack and how much she loved him, images of their wedding day and walks along the beach with the dogs flashing in her mind. She pictured the bakery and happy mornings gathered around the dining room with Pamela and Trudy, working hard together and also enjoying their company. She imagined her parents, feeling an ache in her chest, as she thought of the moment someone would make the devastating call to them that their daughter had been killed.

"Goodbye, Meghan," Erin laughed as she held the gun to Meghan's face and pulled the trigger.

24

——————

When Erin pulled the trigger, Meghan heard the sinister sound of the metal click, followed by cursing. She opened her eyes. Erin was fiddling with the gun, and a furious look on her face.

"What happened?" she muttered as she took the gun apart and studied the barrel. "Why didn't it work?"

"The gun malfunctioned," Meghan thought as she looked left and right, trying to identify an escape path. "I'm *alive*."

Erin was cursing like a sailor, the foul words spilling out of her mouth as though she were vomiting them. Meghan took a slow step forward. Erin did not realize she had moved.

"If I can move a few feet to the left, I can make a run for the front door," she thought as she eyed the exit. James' body was lying next to the door, and she shuddered as she saw the blood pooling around him.

Just then, Erin looked up at her, her eyes flashing. "Not so fast," she ordered, pushing the parts of the gun back into place. "Where do you think you're going?"

She raised the gun again, but before Meghan could speak,

the front door burst open and the police darted in. "Put your hands on your head!" an officer screamed as Erin dropped the gun.

Meghan put her hands on her own head. "She shot him," she yelled as the police snapped a pair of handcuffs on Erin's wrists. "She shot James Kittle in cold blood."

The officer picked up her walkie talkie and called for a paramedic. As Erin was led outside, a team of responders rushed in with a gurney, carefully hoisting James onto the stretcher. Meghan was relieved to see him stir. James was *alive*.

She went to his side and took his hand as the paramedics strapped him to the gurney. "Stay with us, James," she whispered, watching as he winced in pain as a responder cut off his shirt to reveal a wound gushing blood.

"I can't believe she did that to me," he muttered. "She tried to kill me. My own fiancée tried to kill me in my own business."

"Ma'am," a paramedic chided her. "You need to step away from the patient. Unless you are a family member, you need to leave him be."

"I am," she lied, knowing it was wrong, but desperately wanting to find out why Erin had tried to kill them both. "I'm family."

The paramedic shot her a look, but then returned to caring for James as Meghan leaned close to him.

"Why did she do it?" she asked as the paramedics tended to the wound, carefully cleaning it and dressing it in preparation for the ambulance ride to the hospital. "What happened, James? I don't understand. Erin seemed so in love with you…"

"You heard her. Erin thought I was a loser," he muttered, a dark look crossing his face. "Though there is much more to it. She used to date Anthony when they were in high school.

Did you know that? She and Anthony were two peas in a pod during sophomore year."

Meghan's jaw dropped. "What?" she cried. "Erin and *Anthony Diggs*? Your partner? Your friend?"

"Yes," he confirmed. "They broke up, as most high school romances do, but Erin never got over it. I always wondered sometimes if she got with me to somehow make *him* mad. Not that he cared about what she did; Anthony had so many women in his life, Erin didn't matter to him."

Meghan was shocked. "So why was Erin so upset about the business? I don't understand."

"She was a silent partner," he admitted. "She wanted the business to take off and for us to become rich. She wanted a big, fancy life. She was mad that Anthony and Bonnie had money; Bonnie had a nice inheritance from her grandparents, and she and Anthony lived a life of luxury. She was angry when I could never quite get there. She was relieved when Anthony died, Meghan. She hated the ways he was hurting our business, and she thought when he passed away, we could fix things."

Meghan bit her lip. "But Anthony's debts weren't easily fixed just because he died."

"Exactly," he agreed. "Anthony's debts didn't die with him, and Erin didn't understand that. Though it seems like she understands it *now...*"

The paramedics shooed Meghan away. "Ma'am, we have to take him now," they told her. "Please go outside."

She obeyed, and she followed the gurney outside as they took James to the ambulance. Meghan looked around. There were police officers everywhere; lights were flashing, a few reporters had gathered, and Erin Rogers was shrieking in the back of a police car. She could not believe her pleasant, exciting date night had turned into such a circus, and she hoped Jack wasn't worried about her.

"Meghan!"

She turned to see her husband sprinting toward her. His suit was soaking wet, and his blonde hair was dripping with water. His face was distraught, and she felt relief as he made his way to her.

"Are you okay?" he cried as he pulled her into his arms. "What happened? I heard shots and called the police. What is going on? Where is James?"

She looked into his bright blue eyes. "Erin Rogers shot James."

"Her fiance? She shot her own fiance? What happened, Meghan?"

"Yes," she told him. "And she tried to kill me. The gun malfunctioned, Jack. It was so scary. She pulled the trigger, and it didn't work. If it had, I would be dead. Erin shot James and then tried to shoot me."

He wrapped her up in his arms and kissed the top of her head. "Why did she do this? Why did she try to kill James and hurt you?"

"She didn't like the way James was running the business," she explained in a broken voice. "And she tried to kill him. She wanted to get rich and live large, and she realized that was never going to happen if she chose a life with James Kittle."

"She couldn't just break up with him and get a new boyfriend? She had to kill him?"

"I guess so."

Jack held her tightly, and the water from his suit started to soak into Meghan's clothes. "Why are you so wet?" she asked. "What happened to *you*? Did you go swimming or something? You are soaking wet, Jack."

He looked down at himself in disgust. "When James ran inside to help you, a huge wave came out of nowhere," he explained. "It pulled the boat out to sea, and I tried to go in after it. It was too late though; it's long gone. I swam back to shore and heard the gunshot. Fortunately my police issue phone was a new waterproof model so I could call the police."

She shook her head. "I don't think it matters much, now," she told him. "James will have a long recovery ahead of him. I don't know if Big Catch will survive this. The business is in trouble, and James' injuries will surely keep him out of the office for a long, long time..."

He looked at his wife. "Let's get out of here," he suggested, taking her hand. "Go give your statements to the police and let's get home. I think we've both had enough new experiences for one day, don't you?"

Meghan looked up at her husband and nodded. "Going home is exactly what I need right now," she told him. "I think that sounds like the best idea I've heard all day."

25

Two days later, Meghan was happier than ever to be back at work at the bakery. She had taken the previous day off to rest and recover after the traumatic incident at Big Catch, but now, she had returned to work and was filling in the girls on what had happened.

"So *Erin* killed Anthony?" Pamela cried as Meghan nodded. "I thought it was his wife, Bonnie."

"I thought it was Marty Workman," Trudy chimed in. "Or Mayor Rose."

Meghan shook her head. "Mayor Rose wanted Anthony dead," she whispered softly. "He hired someone to do it, but the plan didn't work. He'll be sitting in jail for a long time for conspiring to have him killed."

Trudy's eyes widened. "I saw in the paper that he announced he will not be seeking reelection," she told them as they sat at one of the little white iron tables in the corner.

"Well, of course not," Pamela cried. "He's going to prison for hiring a killer to off Anthony."

"He'll be acquitted," Trudy said primly. "I'm sure of it."

Pamela scowled. "Even if he is, his reputation is ruined,"

she argued. "He won't ever be able to show his face in town again."

"Who will be the mayor, then?" Meghan asked.

"Why don't you run?" Trudy said excitedly. "You always have good ideas, and you are a young, cute thing."

"Politics is not for me," Meghan assured them. "I'm happy right here, with you."

The little silver bells chimed and Karen walked in.

"What about Karen?" Trudy wondered as she approached the table and threw her arms around Meghan.

"I had to see if you were okay," Karen cried, kissing Meghan on the cheek. "I heard about what that woman almost did to you. How terrible."

Meghan smiled. "I'm okay," she promised her friends. "Karen, we were just chatting about the mayoral election."

"I saw Rose isn't planning to run," Karen added, her eyes large. "Who do you think will do it?"

The three women looked at her, each with a smile on their face. "We were thinking you would be a good fit for the job," Meghan grinned. "You are brilliant, brave, bold, and have the energy of a teenager. I think you are just what this town needs, Karen."

Karen blushed. "I don't know about that," she argued. "I don't know if Sandy Bay could keep up with me."

"Will you think about it?" Pamela asked, folding her hands into a prayer. "We need you, Karen. Please?"

Karen laughed. "We'll see," she told them, though Meghan noticed an extra sparkle in her eyes. "Now, tell me about what happened at Big Catch. Meghan, are you sure you are okay?"

Meghan recounted the experience, and Karen gasped. "Why would Erin Rogers do something like that?" she murmured. "To you? And to her fiance? And to Anthony?"

"There's even more that came out," Meghan told Karen

and the ladies. "It turns out, Erin and Anthony were having an affair."

"Didn't you say they were together years ago? In high school?" Pamela asked, her eyes huge with curiosity.

"Yes, they were," Meghan confirmed. "And somehow, they rekindled things behind James' and Bonnie's backs. Erin was having an affair with Anthony, and she wanted to do away with James and Bonnie. She wanted to be the wife of a mayor, and she wasn't going to let Bonnie or James get in the way of that. Anthony refused to go along with it; he may have cheated on his wife repeatedly, but he loved her, in his own way. Anyway, he didn't want her to be killed, and he refused to help Erin. He threatened to tell James what was going on if Erin didn't stop talking about killing his wife."

"Whoa," Trudy muttered.

"Erin snuck into the town hall on the day Anthony died," she continued. "She told the police that she went to hug him for good luck, and she managed to strangle him before he could get away. He died right there in front of her."

"She's a monster," Karen sighed. "I'm so glad you're okay, Meghan. You could have been her next victim."

"I was close," Meghan agreed. "And so was James. Thankfully, his injuries are not major; the bullet went through his chest and out the other side of him. No major organs were pierced, and with some physical therapy, he will be okay."

"That poor man," Trudy clucked. "He lost his best friend, his fiancée tried to kill him, and now, he'll lose his business…"

Meghan smiled. "There is some good news about that," she told the group. "Now that the police know Erin killed Anthony, his life insurance money will go to Bonnie. She is going to run the store with James as her partner."

"That's great," Pamela grinned. "They would make a cute couple, wouldn't they?"

Meghan laughed. "I don't think they're thinking about that quite yet; it's still a bit soon," she insisted. "But apparently, Anthony had been worried about Erin acting out, and he increased his life insurance only a week before he died. It's enough money to keep the business running and to ensure Bonnie is taken care of."

Karen smiled. "What a relief," she cried. "It's all going to work out okay."

Pamela scowled. "Not for us, though," she complained, folding her arms over her chest. "Erin's wedding was going to bring so much money into the bakery, and now, we're left with nothing. How are we going to break into the wedding industry without her big day?"

Meghan shook her head. "It's okay," she promised. "We'll figure it out. There will be more weddings for us to nab, I promise. Besides, it's not even Valentine's Day yet. It's still engagement season. Surely another bride will venture in soon looking for a cake."

"I hope so," Pamela pouted, and the ladies laughed.

"So everything is back to normal now," Karen observed. "James is going to get better, Big Catch is going to survive, and we can all go back to business as usual."

"Wait," Trudy stopped her. "Is everything back to normal at your house, Meghan? Is your awful mother-in-law still camped out there?"

Meghan giggled. "Sarah isn't so bad," she assured them. "In fact, she and I became good friends while she was here."

"Was?" Karen asked. "Is she gone already? I didn't get a chance to spend time with her."

"Sarah left this morning," Meghan explained. "She thought Jack, and I needed some time to ourselves while I processed what happened, and she graciously left after breakfast."

Trudy's eyes widened. "That was so nice of her," she

commented. "It sounds like you two really were able to make things work between you."

Meghan thought of the way her relationship with Sarah had grown over the last few days. While the visit had been rocky at first, she had grown to adore her mother-in-law, and she was sad to see her go.

"I didn't give Sarah enough credit," she admitted. "She is a kind, loving woman, and with my own mom being so uptight and snooty, having a warm mother-figure in my life is something I just wasn't used to. Now that Sarah has come and visited and I've grown accustomed to her, I am so glad we were able to get close."

"A mother-daughter bond is so special," Karen agreed. "Especially when it happens between a mother and daughter-in-law."

"Yes, it is," Meghan grinned as she sat back in her chair. "It's truly sweet."

The End

AFTERWORD

Thank you for reading Velvet Cake and Murder. I really hope you enjoyed reading it as much as I had writing it!

If you have a minute, please consider leaving a review on Amazon, GoodReads and/or Bookbub.

Many thanks in advance for your support!

APPLE PIE AND TROUBLE

CHAPTER 1 SNEEK PEEK

ABOUT APPLE PIE AND TROUBLE

Released: April, 2019
Series: Book 1 – Sandy Bay Cozy Mystery Series

Meghan Truman always had a dream to become a Hollywood actress. Hollywood decided she wasn't good enough. She left Hollywood broken but with a burning desire to start afresh in the Pacific Northwest, pursuing her second dream – opening a bakery.

She never expected that the owner of a rival establishment would be found dead and all eyes would be focused on her as the prime suspect.

As the new girl in town with a new bakery store, she's determined to clear her name and find the murderer; otherwise she'll have to leave Sandy Bay penniless and pitiful and possibly the murderer's next victim.

CHAPTER 1 SNEEK PEEK

"GOOD MORNING, MEGHAN TRUMAN! It's a beautiful day to be in Sandy Bay."

Meghan smiled sleepily at Karen, her seventy-two year old friend and former neighbor, who had just walked through the front door of the bakery, *Truly Sweet*. The two had met back in Los Angeles; Karen was a retired nurse, and she and Meghan had lived in the same apartment complex. Meghan adored Karen's enthusiasm and vigor, and Karen was filled with energy as she burst through the door.

"Someone's cheerful this morning." she said, rubbing her hazel eyes and stifling a yawn as Karen hoisted herself up to sit on the counter. "I wasn't expecting you. I'm sorry I'm still in my pajamas."

Karen tossed her frosted, shoulder-length blonde hair behind her shoulder and shook her head. "Sorry to surprise you, sweetie. I just couldn't resist stopping by. I was driving by after leaving the gym, and I saw that you had painted the front door. I just *had* to stop by and admire it."

Meghan grinned. "I couldn't sleep last night, and so there

I was, outside, painting the front door at two in the morning. I just wanted everything to be perfect,Karen. It's not every day that you start the business of your dreams."

Karen's eyes became solemn and as she nodded, Meghan saw her eyes begin to glitter with tears. "Meghan," she said. "I'm just so proud of you. At twenty-seven years old, you've moved across the country, and now, you're about to open your bakery. How fabulous!"

Meghan walked over to Karen and wrapped her arms around the older woman, feeling the warmth of her body as she leaned her head on Karen's shoulder. "You are too much. I wouldn't be here in Sandy Bay without your help; if you hadn't convinced me to leave LA, I would probably still be at some audition, still trying to make it as an actress."

Karen shrugged her narrow, but muscular shoulders as she gently pulled away from Meghan's embrace. "Look, sweetie," she said kindly. "You are young and beautiful, and the world is your oyster right now. Hollywood is a rough town for such a sweet girl. I think you'll be happier here than you've ever been. Sandy Bay is quiet, and the people are kind. The Pacific Northwest is a special place, Meghan, and I know you'll fit right in."

Meghan ran a hand through her dark, messy hair and sighed. She had another long, busy day ahead of her. After moving to Sandy Bay from Los Angeles on a whim three weeks ago, Meghan's life had been brimming with excitement; Karen had persuaded her to lease a charming little two-story brick building on the town square, and Meghan had applied for the permits to open Truly Sweet, the bakery of her dreams. She had moved her belongings into the tiny upstairs apartment above the bakery, and she had changed her address at the post office. After nearly three years of trying to make it in Hollywood, Meghan was now officially a resident of Sandy Bay, and as she painted and cleaned in preparation for the opening of her bakery, she felt herself begin to feel at ease for the first time since she had left home in Texas after college.

Karen lifted her arms above her body and stretched. "Meghan? Are you sure you don't want to go to pilates with me? There's an afternoon class today, and plenty of girls your age go. It could be a good chance to meet people in Sandy Bay."

Meghan raised one eyebrow at Karen and shook her head. "Karen," she began, "It's nice of you to ask me, but I have to tell you the same thing I told you when you first asked me last night. I've been moving boxes and painting for days, and my body is aching. I can hardly move, let alone do pilates."

Karen shrugged. "Just had to ask," she said. "Well, I'll let you wake up a bit and get your day started. I just had to compliment you on the front door. The yellow paint looks simply fabulous."

Karen leaned in to kiss Meghan on the cheek, and then, she marched out of the bakery, her matching velour sweatsuit lighting up the gray morning as she strode to her orange jeep.

"That lady is in better shape than *me*, and I'm half her age." Meghan murmured to herself as she looked down at her curvy, womanly figure. "I hope I have that much energy when I am in my seventies, because I definitely don't have any today."

Meghan slowly made her way upstairs to change into her clothes, her legs and arms sore from the labor she had put into making Truly Sweet beautiful. As she came back downstairs, she grinned as she stepped into the bakery. She was proud of her hard work; she had little experience with decor or design, but with Karen's help, she had turned the dilapidated brick building into a quaint little space. The walls were painted pale yellow, and little white tables were positioned around the dining area. The counters and cabinets were painted white as well, and a long, painted wooden shelf held a diverse array of rich, green succulents that gave the room a fresh, airy feeling.

"It's almost ready," Meghan said, as she stood in the bakery, her hands on her hips. "It's almost *my* time to shine!"

Meghan took a long breath as she surveyed the pale yellow walls of the bakery. "These could use another coat of paint," she muttered to herself, inhaling deeply. "I could probably get away with the walls as they are, but another coat would be just perfect. We only have three days until the opening though...."

Meghan took a seat at one of the little white tables and looked around the room. She had poured herself into making Truly Sweet a lovely place, and she hoped the citizens of Sandy Bay would be pleased by the addition of a bakery. Back in Los Angeles, Karen had sworn to Meghan that opening a bakery in Sandy Bay would be a wonderful idea, and now, with only a few days until the grand opening, Meghan felt her heart flutter with nerves each time she imagined someone stepping inside and having a taste of Meghan's homemade treats.

"It'll be *awesome*, Meghan. Just imagine it!" Karen had gushed back in California. "Sweetie, you've been auditioning nonstop for every movie, play, and commercial, and I can see it in your eyes that you're unhappy. You always talk about that bakery you worked at in your hometown as a girl, and I see the way your face lights up when you bring a new little dessert over to show me. I'm moving home to Sandy Bay at the end of the month. Come with me. There's a cute little building downtown that's been sitting vacant, and *you* could start a new chapter with a bakery. Just imagine!"

Meghan thought back to that conversation with Karen. It felt like ages ago, but in reality, she had only been in Sandy Bay for a few weeks. Meghan was nervous about the bakery's opening ceremony, but as she studied the little space she had devoted herself to fixing up, she felt her heart pound with pride.

"It's going to be great," she whispered. "I've loved making this place pretty, and if it weren't for Karen, I would still be back trying to make it big in LA. This is where I belong now. This is going to be *home*."

A loud pounding at the front door of the bakery stirred Meghan from her wistful daydreaming, and she nearly jumped out of her seat.

"Hello?" she called out. "Who is it?"

"This is Norman Butcher! Who are *you*?"

Meghan cringed at the loud, fussy voice on the other side of her newly painted door. She rose from the chair, and tucked her dark hair behind her ears.

"It's Meghan. Meghan Truman? I'm new in town."

Meghan carefully pulled the white lace curtains back and peered outside. A short, stout man wearing a pair of tortoise-shell spectacles looked back at her, and he gestured feverishly toward the door.

"Please, open this door. We need to have a chat, Ms. Truman."

Meghan noticed a British accent. She opened the door, and the man came barreling in.

"I see from the sign that was put up outside that this is a bakery," he said brusquely as he took a seat in one of the little white chairs. "I own a tea shop just across the way, and we bake and sell our own goods."

Meghan joined Norman at the table. "Another business owner? How nice of you to stop by." she said happily.

Norman shook his head vigorously. "This isn't a social call," he said sternly as Meghan's eyes widened. "You're new in town, and when I saw that someone was trying to open a bakery here, I knew I needed to speak up."

Meghan shook her head. "I'm not trying to open a bakery here," she said steadily, folding her hands delicately in front of her on the table. "I *am* opening a bakery here. I have all of the paperwork and permits ready, and as soon as I'm finished fixing this place up, I'll be in business."

Norman folded his arms across his chest. He was an older gentleman, and as he furrowed his brow, the wrinkles on his forehead cut deep across his face to form an angry expression. "Look," he said quietly as Meghan leaned away from him. "This town doesn't *need* another place to buy baked goods. It could be years before your business makes a profit. You look young enough. Why don't you go somewhere else and open a bakery? I hear Nantucket is nice."

Meghan rose from the table, irritated with Norman's intrusion. She had work to do, and he was being quite rude.

"Thank you for stopping by today, but I must say goodbye for now," she said, her hazel eyes filled with annoyance as she gestured toward the yellow door of

Truly Sweet. "I'll be staying in Sandy Bay. I do hope we can get along well together."

Norman muttered under his breath as he stomped out, and as he stepped across the threshold, Meghan turned the lock on the door.

"That's *enough* excitement for one morning," she huffed, trying to lower her shoulders and relax her body. She was confused by Norman's visit; everyone she had met in Sandy Bay thus far had been so kind, but Norman's visit was perplexing. He had been terribly rude, and Meghan did her best to not get upset.

Turning back to face the kitchen, she shrugged. "Time to get back to work!" she exclaimed, picking up a paintbrush and smiling as she got underway. She wondered if there would be any other distractions that morning.

You can order your copy of **Apple Pie and Trouble** at any good online retailer.

Apple Pie and Trouble

AMBER CREWES

ALSO BY AMBER CREWES

The Sandy Bay Cozy Mystery Series

Apple Pie and Trouble

Brownies and Dark Shadows

Cookies and Buried Secrets

Donuts and Disaster

Éclairs and Lethal Layers

Finger Foods and Missing Legs

Gingerbread and Scary Endings

Hot Chocolate and Cold Bodies

Ice Cream and Guilty Pleasures

Jingle Bells and Deadly Smells

King Cake and Grave Mistakes

Lemon Tarts and Fiery Darts

Muffins and Coffins

Nuts and a Choking Corpse

Orange Mousse and a Fatal Truce

Peaches and Crime

Queen Tarts and a Christmas Nightmare

Rhubarb Pie and Revenge

Slaughter of the Wedding Cake

Tiramisu and Terror

Urchin Dishes and Deadly Wishes

Velvet Cake and Murder

NEWSLETTER SIGNUP

Want **FREE** COPIES OF FUTURE **AMBER CREWES**
BOOKS, FIRST NOTIFICATION OF NEW RELEASES,
CONTESTS AND GIVEAWAYS?

GO TO THE LINK BELOW TO SIGN UP TO THE
NEWSLETTER!

www.AmberCrewes.com/cozylist

Made in the USA
Coppell, TX
17 March 2021

51896201R00105